Claiming Their Mate

By Paige McKellan

Red-hot animal attraction.

Jules Kingston is a WereLion destined to be the next Lioness of the White Sands Pride. Her fathers, having decided to step down as Leos, have put out a call for a pair of lions to mate with their daughter. Before settling down with mates and a litter of cubs, though, Jules wants to spread her wings.

Of all the Lions in the Pride, Gabriel and Lucas Beckett are the only two who make her panties wet—and the last two she would ever take on as mates. When the brothers stake their claim, she runs, cursing her hormones for reacting to such prime specimens of her species.

Gabe and Luke have known for years that Jules is meant to be their mate. The trick will be to convince their woman she belongs to them. As expected, Jules leads them on a merry chase.

Then a mate fight and hunt is called by a rival pair. To win Jules as their own, Gabe and Luke must prove their dominance over the Pride—and their woman.

Warning: Contains explicit sex, graphic language, stubborn men, an independent woman and red-hot romance.

Rachel's Totem

By Marie Harte

Mountain man or mountain lion? In his case—one and the same.

When Rachel arrives in Cougar Falls for a reading of her aunt's will, she finds herself in a typical mountain town. Except that it's not quite...typical. It's full of the requisite, rough-hewn mountaineers, but these men seem more animal than man.

And one of the rude strangers brings out the animal in her during an embarrassingly orgasmic—and scorching—sexual encounter in an alley. The fantastic tales that the townsfolk tell about the Ac-Taw, a clan of people who can shift into animals, are nothing but folklore. Or are they?

Burke is stunned by his response to Rachel, and even more so when she innocently shows signs of possessing Ac-Taw blood. And this puts her in more danger than she knows, danger that only increases the urgency to mark her as his own.

Rachel comes to realize she's inherited much more than just property. She has also inherited a destiny to protect her newfound home.

For the Ac-Taw aren't just legend—they're real.

Warning, this title contains the following: graphic language, ménage a trois, growling, and hot, steamy sex between Shifters in love :)

Feral Attraction

A SAMHAIN PUBLISHING, LTD. publication.

Samhain Publishing, Ltd.
577 Mulberry Street, Suite 1520
Macon, GA 31201
www.samhainpublishing.com

Editing by Angela James
Cover by Anne Cain

Claiming Their Mate, ISBN 1-59998-915-8
First Samhain Publishing, Ltd. electronic publication: April 2008
Rachel's Totem, ISBN 1-59998-917-4
First Samhain Publishing, Ltd. electronic publication: April 2008
First Samhain Publishing, Ltd. print publication: January 2009

Contents

Claiming Their Mate

Paige McKellan

~9~

Rachel's Totem

Marie Harte

~111~

Claiming Their Mate

Paige McKellan

Chapter One

Usually a pint of Cherry Garcia ice cream made all seem right and put her back in focus, back on track, giving her comfort the way saturated fat and refined sugar was supposed to. As she sat sulking in her bed amid more pillows than there was almost room for, Jules scraped the last remaining bite from the bottom of a second pint of Cherry Garcia and realized no amount of ice cream in the world was going to make things better. Disgusted, she tossed the empty container on her nightstand, adding it to the pile of candy wrappers, crumpled chip bags and an empty jar of olives.

Thank God she had a good metabolism.

Jules knew who was to blame for the late night binge that had her stomach pitching and rolling. She'd like to blame Martin and David Marshall. And Will and John Reynolds. Or Harlan and Mitch Payton. She'd *really* like to blame them. In fact she would love to place the blame on the entire male population of the White Sands Pride but she couldn't. All the men who had been pursuing her the past three months, and driving her crazy in the process, were doing what came naturally as a matter of tradition and their DNA. No, the men at fault were her fathers and there wasn't a damn thing she could do about it.

In three short months her life had gone from normal and pleasant to whacked out and shitty. When her fathers, Dane and Marcus Kingston, announced they were stepping down as Leos of the White Sands Pride, a call had gone out to all the unattached male Lions under their domain and Jules found her life turned upside down. The hounds of hell, or rather the Lions of her hell, had been hard on her paws, trying to persuade her to accept a mating she wasn't ready for and didn't want. However, what she wanted didn't matter.

She belonged to a clan of WereLions, a fierce breed of shape shifters, and she was bound by the laws and customs her society had embraced since recorded time. Having no brothers and as the eldest of three daughters, it was her duty to mate with a pair of WereLions and continue the Kingston line by bearing sons who would lead the Pride into the future. A member of the Kingston family had led the Pride for over two hundred years, a right of succession her fathers refused to abandon.

She was twenty-three and had her life ahead of her. Every time she thought about the future and the responsibility of carrying on the family lineage, she had thought in terms of years, very many, very long years, before she had to step up, accept a mating pair and birth the cubs of the next generation of Leos. Her fathers' announcement and resulting mate call had put a stop to her plans of leaving the Pride for a while and seeing the world.

For the hundredth time in the past three months she cursed herself for returning home right after college instead of taking time to explore the world and be on her own. She had come back after school for two reasons. The first was because she'd missed her family. Setting aside the fact she wasn't speaking to any of them right now, they were a close family and their separation during her years in school had been difficult.

She'd wanted to spend time in the comfort of her home surrounded by her parents and sisters.

Not so much anymore.

Jules wanted to be as far away from Logan, New Mexico as she could be, communicating only by postcard, and even that would be done begrudgingly.

The second reason she had come back was because of the Pride, and because the freedoms she had in Logan she wouldn't have elsewhere. She was a WereLion who needed to shift and roam and prowl like her body demanded, giving over to the more elemental side of her being. There were some Non-Weres living in Logan and the surrounding area but not many. Of the full humans living alongside the Pride, only some knew their secret—those whose families had lived here for generations—the rest remained oblivious as most humans do to things they don't believe are real or possible. Here she could shift and roam the ranch or other sanctioned ranges safely, something she had missed while away at school. Now, being home and around others of her kind was a pain-in-the-ass problem and not the blessing it was supposed to be.

Jules didn't want one husband, much less two. Not now at least. Years ago she'd accepted her fate as the next Lioness of the Pride. Jules knew she would be mated to the next Leos. She had planned to leave the Pride for a while then return, maybe in ten years or so, and accept her role as future Lioness and select her mates. On her terms and in her own time. Not her fathers'. The Pride operated much in the same way those in the wild did; two male leaders mated to one female. Two Leos rather than one helped ensure the safety and continuity of the Pride and their lineage. The mating pair would be brothers or men of the same bloodline. Her friends from outside the Pride would be shocked to learn she would have two husbands. Knowing she would share her bed with more than one man should scare her.

13

Actually it was quite the opposite.

Thinking about taking two men to mate and to her bed made her hot and wet. Not that she wanted to deal with the attitudes of two Leos who would most likely try to keep her under their control; the amount of testosterone one male WereLion in his prime had was staggering. Having to put up with two Lions would drive her crazy. Jules envisioned many arguments in her future as she had no intention of letting any one man control her, much less two. But the tantalizing thought of having two strong men to pleasure her was another matter, something she knew she wouldn't resist. Ever since her fathers had made their announcement, she'd been consumed with thoughts of lying in the dark, in her bed, between two men intent on staking a claim. The images running through her mind had her squirming under the covers until her panties were damp.

And it wasn't just two nameless faces she saw on the men who would hold her and stroke her and claim her as their own for all time. When she closed her eyes and imagined being held between her future mates, she always saw the same two faces.

Gabriel and Lucas Beckett.

Two men she would never, ever, *ever* consider as mates.

No matter how much they got her juices flowing and made her want to purr.

With those two she would never stand a chance of retaining her independence. Gabe and Luke would control every second of her life until she was ready to scream and escape. Or claw them to death. Just thinking about the two men and their commanding ways set her mind burning in resentment. They were demanding, controlling and arrogant.

And two of the most gorgeous men she had ever seen.

Most of the Pride, both male and female, were good looking,

but hands down the Beckett brothers were the best looking of all.

Too bad just the thought of them had her hackles rising. If she were in Lion form, her tail would be twitching in aggravation.

Thankfully she didn't have to worry about the Becketts answering the call. While Luke ran his family's ranch, which bordered her fathers' spread, Gabe was an active member of the Navy, a U.S. Navy Seal. Since it took two men to take over a Pride, and she had heard through the grapevine that Gabe was planning on a long career in the Navy, there was no way they could mate her. Yay her. While her body might want them, her common sense and self-preservation ruled them out. Even with them out of the running she still had way too many eager Lions to deal with.

Damn her fathers for putting her in this mess.

Not that she didn't put part of the blame on the men who had been pursuing her. They really needed to learn to take no for an answer. But as typical males, and the proud cats that marked their DNA, they were doing what was natural in trying to take control of the Pride and become the next Leos. The problem was that most of them were jerks and incapable of running the Pride, but that didn't stop them from thinking they could. Attitude and confidence were synonymous with WereLions. If a man could shift between human form and lion form he was bound to have plenty of attitude in any form.

Jules had had enough of the smarmy comments, lewd suggestions and invasion of her personal space. And the sniffing, she was *so* done with the sniffing. If one more man tried to sniff her she would scream. She couldn't go anywhere, not even to the grocery store to stock up on comfort food, without running into a pair of potential mates determined to convince her why they would be her best choice.

The herd was thinning though. Just like in the wild, the Lions were eliminating their competition, fighting it out amongst themselves, scaring each other off for the right to approach her and present their case. On one hand she was grateful the pool of potential mates was getting smaller but that relief was short lived. As their numbers dwindled it meant her time was running out and her situation was about to heat up. Her potential mates would begin putting more pressure on her to make a decision.

She'd managed to run off a few pairs already but Jules didn't know how much longer that would last. As much as she resented being in this position now, at this stage of her life, she understood the importance and the responsibility that came with it. Not only was she selecting her future mates, her life partners until her death, but these men she would take into her bed and into her body would be the next Leos, men who would be charged with leading the Pride. It was an awesome responsibility. Her fathers would have the final approval of her choice. It was their duty to see the Pride protected. So far she had been fortunate the decision had not already been made for her. The Leos, like leaders of other Prides had done, could have ordered her into a mating of their choosing and she would have been honor-bound to accept it.

Accept it or leave the Pride and her heritage behind.

She could continue to dwell on this all night and still not find a solution she could live with. Since she had to be up early, Jules shut off the light and settled deeper under her covers, wishing her stomach would stop churning and her mind would stop running. Her last thought before she fell asleep was that she should have bought one more pint of Cherry Garcia. Stomachache be damned.

He'd missed this. Running at full speed in his true form, his powerful stride eating up the ground as he gave in to his beast and roared loud and fierce into the night, re-staking his claim on the land. His muscles bunched under his skin as he ran through the warm night air. It had been too long since he had shifted. Too long since he'd been home. The hot, dry climates of Iraq and Afghanistan were similar but those lands had not been home. The moment he'd driven back into his territory, the smell of the sand and soil called him to shift and leave his mark.

Gabe had wanted to come sooner, as soon as he had received the call from the Leos, but Uncle Sam didn't set its clock to the demands of the Pride. It had taken three months to resign his commission and settle his affairs, ending his ten-year career in the Navy. A decision he had made quickly and without reservation. His commanding officers had tried their best to convince him to stay on for another tour but he hadn't changed his mind. He would miss the brotherhood of his fellow SEALs and the honor it had been serving his country, but his Leos had called. His fealty belonged to his Pride.

His Pride.

His and Luke's.

Gabe slowed his body, reining in his muscles until his speed decreased, walking quietly to the fence at the edge of his property. Their ranch, the Roaring Lion, bordered the Kingston operation, the Double K. He wanted nothing more than to jump the fence and mark the Double K with his scent. Mark the land and the woman sleeping unaware inside the house up on the hill.

He had come home for her.

Jules Kingston would be his and Luke's mate.

The decision had already been made.

His chest rumbled in a satisfied purr as he walked the fence. He couldn't act on his instinct to claim and mate, not without Luke. His brother was back at the house, waiting for him to return. Luke understood his need to shift and roam the ranch. His brother had reaped the rewards of staying on the ranch and running the place when his parents retired years ago. Luke shifted as he pleased and gave over to his baser nature whenever he could. He could hunt and roam and exert his instincts. Serving in the Navy and the places he had traveled and lived had not afforded Gabe the opportunity to shift as often as his body demanded. Now that he was home, he could give in to his needs. Gabe threw back his head and let loose one last mighty roar, then turned and headed back to the house and his brother.

Luke was waiting for him in the barn. With a sigh of regret Gabe shifted back to his human form, the transformation not nearly as satisfying as shifting into his Lion's body. The horses in their stalls didn't even whinny at the change; they were used to Lions roaming the ranch and sharing their space.

Gabe gave a grunt of thanks to his brother as he dressed in the jeans, shirt and boots he'd brought him.

"You're welcome." Luke understood his grunts. "Feel better?"

"Yeah, I do. Sorry about leaving like that but it's been a long time." Gabe sat on a bale of hay and pulled on his boots. "Did you leave me anything to eat?"

"There's a plate in the oven; steaks and baked potatoes. I ate all the cake."

There wasn't much he could say about that so the brothers

left the barn and headed for the house. "Fill me in on where we stand."

Luke matched his long stride to Gabe's. "The Leos are very happy you made it home. I called them earlier, told them you were back and we're ready to make our move. Things have started to pick up around here and they have just about run out of patience with the situation. Jules has refused to cooperate, just like they predicted she would. They are not happy about the way she's been acting toward the pairs asking for her. She's managed to run some off but not many. Dominance fights have started."

"Shit," Gabe cursed under his breath as they entered the house through the kitchen door. He knew the interest in her would be high but he and Luke could handle it; Jules Kingston was a beautiful woman and that, coupled with control of the Pride as her dowry, made her a very desirable mate. Yeah, he and Luke would take care of their competition but he was pissed they might have to take time away from her claiming to do it. If their brothers in the Pride were smart, they would stand down and step aside when they heard the news, if not they would learn quickly the consequences of challenging their future Leos. "I bet she's been causing trouble. The Leos should never have put out the call until I made it back. This could have been over and done with quickly."

Gabe wasn't happy that Dane and Marcus had announced their plans at the last Pride gathering. It gave the other Lions three months to try and stake their claim. Not that he or Luke had any doubt they would come out victorious and take over the Pride, but by announcing before he was home, Jules had had three months to get her back up and dig in her heels. What she didn't know was their mating her was a done deal and had been for three years.

Luke grabbed a couple beers out of the fridge as Gabe got

his plate, piled high with three thick blood-rare steaks and two baked potatoes, from the oven. His stomach growled; shifting and running always made him hungry.

"Jules is not happy about this." Twisting the cap off his beer, Luke took a seat across from Gabe. "I saw her sister, Marine, in town yesterday. She says Jules isn't talking to any of them. She's pissed her fathers are doing this now. Doesn't understand why they're stepping down while they're still in their prime. Marine said she looks ready to bolt."

Gabe took a long draw on his own beer. Jules bolting was the reason her fathers had decided to step down. When she graduated from college her plan had been to stay awhile, visit with her family, then leave the Pride for a few years. With her Masters degree in computer science she could work anywhere. It was no secret she wanted to spread her wings before assuming her role as Lioness. The Leos made the announcement when they did because Jules was getting ready to leave. Dane and Marcus had told him they could see how restless she was and they were afraid if she left she wouldn't come back. Or if she did come back she wouldn't fulfill her duty to accept her mates and breed the next Leos.

Jules was a stubborn one. She hated anyone telling her what to do. He had never met a woman more in need of a good spanking than her. Even when she was a kid, coming over to play with their sister Jenna, she was all sass and spunk. The few times he'd seen her during her teen years, confidence and attitude radiated from her in droves. She should have grown out of it but the last time he'd seen her, three years ago, she was as mouthy as ever. The only difference was she wasn't a little girl anymore. The smart-mouthed cub had grown into a beautiful, tempting woman. A hellcat destined to drive him and Luke crazy. Gabe acknowledged the defiance and attitude were part of her appeal as was her sharp mind and quick thoughts.

The smart mouth he could have done without but it was part of her package, a package he and Luke would take. She had been raised to accept her role in the Pride but that didn't mean she was going to go quietly along with their plans.

"What has she been up to?" he asked his brother.

Luke smiled. "Well," he drawled, "it depends on who she's trying to get rid of. Her tongue is as sharp as ever. She told the Marshall brothers she would never consider them as mates because they were incapable of keeping their dicks in their pants. With the Reynolds brothers she whined and bitched about everything under the sun, which had them running because it reminded them too much of their mother. She slapped Chad and Chris Davis when they tried to sniff her. And, this is my favorite by the way, tonight she hit Mitch Peyton with her car at Stouffer's Market."

"She what?" Gabe gasped out around a chuckle.

"It seems he and his cousin Harlan were trying to convince her to give them a test run. According to Lou Ann Stouffer who called Jenna and then Jenna who called me, Jules took offense at the Peyton boys' suggestion of going back to Mitch's place to see how it felt to be fucked by two Lions in their prime. They promised her the experience would be so mind shattering it would put an end to this business and make her decision easier." The light faded from Luke's eyes and his jaw hardened as he went on. "She fended them off and made it to her car but when Mitch blocked her exit she got fed up and rammed him. Lou Ann said both his legs broke from the impact. By the time he shifted to heal then shifted back, Jules was speeding down the road. It's time for this to be over, Gabe."

The anger in his brother's eyes matched his own. This was getting out of hand. Jules knew how to protect herself and no member of the Pride would ever hurt her or their life would be

21

forfeit, but that didn't mean she should have to put up with this shit. This was why he had tried to convince her fathers to put off the announcement and mate call until he could get out of the service.

By Pride Law, Luke alone could not have pursued her as a mate; he had to wait for Gabe to return. It took two adult male Lions to stake a claim on a future Lioness and the reins of the Pride. The brothers understood why their Leos had made the announcement when they did even though they both wished they hadn't. If Jules was ready to run, her fathers should have let her. The Beckett brothers would have found her and brought her back. Of that there was no doubt.

Three years ago when Jules had been home on Christmas break and Gabe had been back on leave, the brothers had taken one look at the woman she'd become and made the decision to mate her. Gabe's cock swelled as he remembered how alluring she was. Her multi-colored mane was long and thick, a mix of golden browns and blondes he itched to sink his hands into. She was beautiful, like most of the women in the Pride, but it was her face with the high cheekbones, straight nose and slightly pointed chin that drew him to her. Young and fresh, her nubile body turned him on like no one else in the Pride ever had. She had long legs that were made to wrap around a man's waist, generous high breasts and an ass just plump enough to fill his hands; an ass that could take a spanking or a fucking, whatever he was in the mood for.

Good looks and a hot body weren't the only reason they wanted her. Because of their ten-year age difference Gabe had never paid much attention to Jules when she was a kid playing with his sister; he'd known she was the Leos' daughter and future Lioness but he hadn't given her much thought. When he saw her, or rather smelled her, as an adult for the first time three years ago, things changed. Her body had ripened until her woman's curves were fully developed, fulfilling their earlier promise, teasing *his* body into a sexual frenzy. During that visit to the ranch, Gabe had taken the time to study her, had approached her, gotten close enough to smell her, and that's when he knew she would be his. His and Luke's.

The brothers had shared women before. They enjoyed the connection and the feel of a woman pressed between them as they slid their cocks into her body, making her beg for more until she panted and screamed in release. The lust in Luke's eyes when he looked at Jules told Gabe his brother was just as eager to claim her and make her theirs.

Three years ago she had been too young to mate but that didn't stop them from staking their claim. Before Gabe returned to duty, he and Luke had met with the Leos and announced their intention of mating her. Her fathers had been pleased with their plans; they knew it would take strong men to lead the Pride after they stepped down and the Beckett brothers were capable of holding the Pride and leading it into the future. Their concerns as Leos overrode their concerns as fathers. By Gabe and Luke mating Jules, her fathers felt confident she and the Pride would be taken care of so they agreed to the mating, fulfilling both duties as Leos and fathers.

The brothers agreed to wait until she was older and done with college before moving forward with the mating. Both he and Luke recognized her spirit and wanted to see her flourish and live a little before settling down. Gabe went back to the service and Luke stayed on the ranch, both men waiting until the time was right to claim their mate.

Gabe pushed his empty plate aside and sat back in his chair, finishing his beer. "You ready for this?" He studied his brother then grinned as Luke's eyes turned darker as lust made its mark. He understood what he saw in Luke's face. His lust was rising as well.

"More than ready," Luke agreed as he finished his own beer.

"Then we move on her tomorrow."

Chapter Two

Jules woke with a headache. By the time she showered, dressed and was walking toward the kitchen, two Advil had taken the edge off but it still lurked right behind her eyes, waiting for the chance to take hold again. She'd woken a few times during the night but had fallen back into a restless kind of sleep that left her feeling cranky and out of sorts.

She had to get her act together because she had a meeting in downtown Logan this morning with the marketing and promotions director of the Logan Chamber of Commerce. Since she'd finished school, she'd been doing freelance work designing websites for local businesses. With her Masters degree in computer science she could have gotten any number of jobs but had settled for freelance work for now, not wanting to tie herself down so when she left she could move on and not feel guilty about leaving a full-time job. Though it didn't look like she would be leaving any time soon, Jules continued with the freelance work, preferring the freedom setting her own schedule afforded her.

As she reached the kitchen, she heard raised voices coming through the open arches and her headache returned in full force. Damn it! Squaring her shoulders when she heard her name bellowed, Jules sucked it up and went in to see what the problem was.

"You hit Mitch Peyton with your car? What were you thinking?" her father roared, sounding more like a Lion than a man.

"Calm down, Dane," her mother said peacefully as she piled mounds of scrambled eggs onto a serving platter. "Shouting at her isn't going to change anything."

"I'm not shouting," he shouted. Her father Dane was the loud one in the family while Marcus was the quiet parent.

"Actually you are. You always shout, Dad," Marine, her youngest sister, chimed in from the kitchen table where she sat buttering a piece of toast. "In fact—" A hard glare from her father shut her down. "Just pointing out the obvious, Dad," she said with a sniff.

"Jules, take the eggs to the table, please. Dane, sit down and eat your breakfast while it's still hot." She shoved the platter into Jules' hands. "Marine, you better eat quickly. You don't want to be late for school."

Jules took the platter to the table and set it down in front of her father Marcus.

"Good morning, Jules. Busy night last night? Your mother and father and I didn't know you went out after dinner." Her father set aside the newspaper. "Is there something you'd like to tell us?" While he wasn't loud like Dane, the steel undertone in his voice told her he too was displeased by what had happened.

Resigned to the inevitable grilling, Jules sat and poured herself a glass of juice. "Who told you?"

Since Logan was a small town and news often traveled fast, it could have been any number of people. Jules didn't think it was either Mitch or his cousin Harlan; if they had been the ones to rat her out they would have had to explain why she ran Mitch over and she didn't think that was a conversation either man wanted to have with her fathers or their Leos.

"Who didn't?" Marine piped up. "The phone has been ringing off the hook all morning. First, Angie Stouffer called; she heard it from her daughter Lou Ann. Then Karen Whitters called; she heard it from Angie. Cal Henry, Jim Banks, and Lori Peters were next. I don't know who they heard it from. The only one who got the story right was Angie. By the time Mom and the Dads got off the phone, Mitch's injuries included two broken legs, two broken arms, a ruptured spleen and claw marks down his face."

Jules blurted the first thing that came to her mind. "How do you know Angie got the story straight?"

"That's what you want to know. That's all you have to say?" Dane roared.

"What your father meant to say, dear," her mother broke in as she set platters of steaks, bacon and hash browns on the table, "is the reason Angie got it right is because it's the same story he heard from Sheriff Thomas who saw what happened as he was pulling into the parking lot. You hit Mitch in the parking lot of Stouffer's Market, broke both his legs then drove off as he shifted and healed. What she didn't say is why you hit him with your car. I believe that is what your fathers and I would like to know."

Jules looked up from her juice glass, which she had been studying as if it were the most interesting thing on earth, and scanned the faces at the table. She ignored Marine and her shitty grin. Her mother had a look of utmost patience on her face tinged with both curiosity and understanding. Her fathers didn't look too happy. Imagine that. Deciding it was better to get this over with, Jules sat back in her chair and faced the inquisition.

"Last night, I had words with Mitch and Harlan. I went to Stouffer's because I wanted some ice cream and ran into them, him...literally. I lost my temper, I know that. I should not have tried to run him over but he pissed me off." Jules ran a hand over her face and brushed her thick hair away from her neck.

She wasn't prepared or willing to discuss exactly what Mitch and Harlan had said to her; it was one thing for her parents and sister to know that she would be sleeping with two men when she was mated but it was an entirely different thing to tell them about being propositioned to a night of preview sex. She didn't want to deal with the shitstorm her fathers would start if they knew about Mitch and Harlan. Since they had no chance in hell of ever being her mates, Jules didn't see the point of making more of a mess of this situation by telling her fathers what they had been up to. But this was too good an opportunity to keep her mouth entirely shut on the situation as a whole.

"This entire thing pisses me off." She looked down from one end of the table to the other at both her fathers. "I don't understand why you decided to step down as Leos. You're both still young and in your prime. I understand and accept my place in the Pride. Yes, I do," she countered when Dane shook his head. "You think just because I want to run free for a while that means I'm going to toss away my heritage. I'm not. You have no idea what it's like to be followed around by every male Pride member who has delusions of grandeur and aspirations of power. I'm sick of it. When I thought of my future, about becoming the next Lioness of the Pride, I always imagined it happening years down the road when I'd be ready to deal with it, not now, not when I'm this young."

"When your mother was your age she had already given birth to you and was pregnant with your sister Nessa." Marcus looked at her in that way he often did, with quiet contemplation while his still-handsome face gave nothing away. "You're done with school and ready to move on, Jules. The Pride is ready to move on as are your father, mother and I."

Frustrated by his lack of answer, Jules waved away the plate her mother had fixed for her. "I know how old Mom was when you mated her. But I'm not Mom. And you still didn't answer my question. Why did you decide to step down now? Are you ill? Is there something you're not telling me? What is it?" When they had made the decision and the announcement, they had done so with no explanation, not even to her. It had pissed her off at the time and still did whenever she thought about it.

"No, we're not ill, Jules," Dane answered with no bite and no roar. "Your father and I have run this Pride for more than thirty years. We took over when your grandfather died and did so with honor. Times have changed since we assumed leadership. Dane and I decided now was the time to step aside and bring new blood into power."

Another non-answer.

Jules made a mental grimace as she realized neither of her fathers was going to share their reasoning. Her mother hadn't been any more forthcoming on the subject than her fathers were. She had been hearing the same thing for three months. That topic may be closed but there was still another one she wanted to address.

"You could have gone about it in a different way. All putting out the mate call did was bring out every jerk ass Lion in the Pride with a taste for power. I'm sick and tired of being confronted ten times a day."

"Are you saying," Marcus started slowly, "you would rather have us choose your mates for you?"

"No." Her answer was strong and immediate.

She wanted no part of an arranged marriage and she knew her fathers could press the issue and take the choice out of her hands. Their decision may be the final one but at least she had been given the opportunity to weed through the masses first and try to find mates that suited her as well as the Pride. What she really wanted was a love match like her parents had. Almost twenty-five years together and she could see the love between her mother and fathers was still as strong as it was the day they mated. That's what she wanted and that's why she'd gone along with the mate call, all in an effort to find love. If she had to do this, to step up and be the next Lioness now instead of later, she'd take her time and try to find a mating pair she could fall in love with and who would love her back the same way.

"Have faith in your fathers, Jules," her mother advised. "I know this is hard, probably the hardest thing you've ever gone through, but it will work out in the end. Now," she added, passing full plates around the table, "I want everyone to eat before the food gets cold."

After that, the subject of her impending mating and the chaos surrounding it was shut down; her mother might have been the soft-spoken one in the family, but that didn't mean she wasn't to be obeyed. Jules could have pressed the matter and started it up again but she didn't. Instead, she deferred to her mother and ate breakfast while she listened to her sister ramble on in the way only teenagers do and her fathers comment on the idiocy of all things teenagers do.

When she got up and put her plate in the sink, her mother reminded her they were having guests for dinner tonight and she should be on time and dressed in something nice. It wasn't until she was in her car on the way to work that she realized no one mentioned who their dinner guests would be.

By the time she made it home it was almost five o'clock. A good part of her day had been taken up correcting the spreading rumors and gossip over what had happened with Mitch at Stouffer's last night. The Pride members knew she was

30

vetting potential mates and were curious about what happened. Like most small towns, gossiping could be considered an occupation and Logan was no different. Her cell had rung constantly until she gave up and shut it off.

Since she'd spent the majority of the day at the Chamber of Commerce working on their website, she had managed to avoid all but a few potential mates. In an effort to quell the speculation on her mental state, she had actually been almost nice to the men she ran into. Points for her, she thought as she ran up the stairs to her room to take a shower. Proud of herself and her earlier attempt at self-control, Jules thought she deserved a reward and decided to drive to Santa Fe for the weekend to visit friends. She would have left tonight but she'd promised her mother she would be here for dinner. First thing in the morning she was heading out for a weekend, alone and potential-mate free.

After her shower, Jules dried her hair and left it flowing around her shoulders then put on a little mascara and lip gloss before getting dressed. Aiming at avoiding an argument with her mother, she passed on her usual attire of jeans and a shirt and put on a sundress. Vain as the next woman, she admitted she looked good; the salmon-colored cotton clung to her curves and ended a few inches above her knees, showing off her pretty, long legs. Living in New Mexico and being a WereLion, she always had a light tan which was displayed nicely by the thin straps holding up the dress, leaving her shoulders bare. Pleased with how she looked, she went downstairs.

She found her mom in the kitchen finishing up the dinner prep. "Anything I can do to help?"

"No thanks, honey. You look nice. You should wear dresses more often." Living on a working ranch, and often working on a working ranch, didn't mix well with dresses and skirts, a fact Cherry Kingston refused to understand.

"Thanks, Mom. So do you." Her mom always looked nice. At forty-seven Cherry still had a good figure, her delicately boned face was wrinkle free and her blonde mane lacked the grey hair full humans often had at her age; WereLions aged more slowly, often looking ten to fifteen years younger than their human counterparts.

Jules picked out a crouton from the salad bowl and sat at the kitchen island. "So, who are we feeding tonight?"

"Lucas Beckett is coming to dinner. Your fathers invited him."

Panic rose in her throat then quickly subsided. No reason to worry, she thought; with Gabe still in the Navy, Lucas Beckett was not in the running as a potential mate. Jules willed away the blush threatening to spread across her cheeks at the idea of sitting across from Luke tonight, especially after the way she'd thought about him and his brother last night. Spending time with one Beckett brother was hard enough; she didn't know if she could handle two.

"Where is everybody?"

"Your sister is on her way home from cheerleading practice and your fathers are in the barn office. Lucas should be here in a few minutes."

The Beckett spread, the Roaring Lion, bordered her fathers' land. While the Double K was a cattle operation, the Roaring Lion raised both cattle and horses. Growing up she had been close friends, was still a close friend, with Jenna, their younger sister, and had spent nearly as much time at their ranch as she had at her own. Because of their age difference Jules had had very little to do with the brothers. Gabe was the older of the two, thirty-three compared to Luke's thirty-one. After college, Gabe had entered the Navy and she'd seen him a few times since then, the last time three years ago at Christmas. Luke she saw more of as he had come back to the family ranch after getting a degree in animal husbandry and business management. Their ranch was nearly as large as her fathers', one of the largest in the state.

Thinking about the Beckett brothers had her thoughts drifting back to her impending mating, not that they were ever far away from the topic. "Mom," she started as she took another crouton, "what's it like being mated to two men?"

Cherry smiled as she poured two glasses of wine from the bottle on the counter and placed one in front of her daughter. "How much do you want to know?"

"What do you mean?"

"Well, there's the aspect of dealing with two very strong, very stubborn men. Then there's the part about running the household of said men and their equally stubborn children. Being Leos is a big part of who your fathers are, so there's that to consider. And then you have the sexual—"

"Not that part, Mom." WereLions were highly sexual creatures and embraced sexuality as a natural part of their lives but hearing about her parents' sex life was just a little too natural for her. Jules took a big drink of her wine, ignoring her mother's light laughter.

"That *part* is an *important* part of my relationship with your fathers, Jules, just like it will be for you with your mates. Having one man cherish and love you can be overwhelming. The thought of two can be downright scary. I know you think this is happening too soon for you and you're not ready to accept the responsibility, but being mated to the right men is a wonderful thing, Jules. It's work pleasing two men *and* yourself, both in and out of the bedroom, I'm not going to lie about that, but the rewards are worth it. I've been with your fathers for almost twenty-five years and every one of them has been happy. That's not to say we don't fight or argue," she added, then paused to drink from her own wine. "There have been nights one or both of your fathers found themselves sleeping in the guest room or on the couch, but overall we've found a balance that works for us and our family." Cherry reached across the counter and took her daughter's hand. "I know part of the reason you're having such a hard time with this mating business is because you're scared, and that's okay, but give your fathers a chance and trust they know what they're doing."

"How did you know they were the right ones? That they were right for you?"

Cherry was quiet for a moment as she considered the question. "You know the Pride is close and the members know each other or at least of each other. I knew your fathers but not very well, since our paths didn't cross often. In fact, I never saw them together until I came back to the Pride after college. I was celebrating my graduation with friends at the Cactus Brand Bar." She smiled over the memory. "From the moment they walked through the door I couldn't take my eyes off them. They were handsome, very good looking, but it was more than their looks that got my attention. The two of them, standing there together as a unit, well, they took my breath away. I was drawn to both of them. They took a table near mine and I had the hardest time concentrating on what my friends were saying. When Dane asked me to dance, I went and when Marcus joined us it felt like we were the only people on the dance floor. Being with the two of them felt right. They made me feel things I'd never felt before. They claimed me and we mated that week and married the next."

Jules thought about what her mother said as she finished off her wine. She had seen firsthand what a great relationship her parents had. Even though she didn't want to think about it, she knew her parents had formed a loving, sexually bonded triad. More than once she had come upon them in an embrace that proved the trio enjoyed their relationship. Her parents loved each other. She wanted nothing less in her own mating.

She set aside her thoughts and picked up the salad bowl when she heard her fathers coming down the hall; the sooner dinner was over, the sooner she could get packed and ready to leave for the weekend and escape this mating business for a while. Jules pasted on what she hoped was a pleasant and welcoming smile before turning to welcome her father and their guest.

If it wasn't for her mother's quick hands the salad would have gone down to the floor, bowl and all.

Chapter Three

"Let me take that, Jules." Cherry rescued the salad and set it on the counter, not missing a step before turning back to her mates and their guests. "Gabriel, it's good to have you home. You've been gone a long time." The hug she gave him was warm and friendly. "Lucas—" she turned to the other man, giving him an equally warm welcome, "—even with you next door I don't see as much of you as I'd like to."

"Thank you, Mrs. Kingston, it's good to be back." Gabe may have been addressing Cherry but Jules was the one he looked at as he spoke. She shifted her gaze between the two brothers, missing what Luke said to her mother, trying to calm the rising panic flooding her body. *No. No, no, no.* Not the Becketts, not Gabe and Luke. Gabe was a career military man. That's what she'd been told; everyone said he was in the Navy for life. With Gabe gone, she should have been safe from him and Luke. Calm down, she needed to calm down. Maybe she was jumping to conclusions and Gabe was home on leave, just here for a visit, not here to stay.

Ignoring the conversation going on without her, Jules realized a couple things. The Beckett brothers were just as imposing and alluring as she remembered. They were handsome men, not just their faces but their bodies too. The brothers were tall, a few inches over six feet, their bodies corded with sleek muscles, their chests wide and powerful. They radiated strength and confidence. It had been three years since she'd seen them together but the reaction she'd had then was the same as the one she had now; just looking at the two brothers made her heart beat faster and her body warm, reminding her she was a woman, but more, a WereLion, with sexual needs and demands her nature would not let her ignore. She didn't react like this to other Lions, certainly not to the pairs who'd been chasing her tail all over town. No, sexual desire and attraction in WereLions was much like it was for humans; attracted to some, indifferent to others. There was nothing indifferent about her reaction to Gabe and Luke.

Three years ago she'd been shocked by her response to these men but smart enough to stay out of their path, despite the pull she'd felt—a pull that still had her dreaming about them when she let her guard down. Something her mother said earlier popped into her head; how her fathers, as a unit, took her breath away. It was the same for her. Separate, these men were a danger to any woman's psyche. Together, they were lethal.

This is not going to happen. She wasn't going to let it. That's when her second realization of the night came to mind; of everyone in the room, she was the only one shocked by Gabe and Luke being here together. Her parents had known Gabe was back. If they knew that, they damn well knew the Becketts were eligible mates. This was the first time her parents had presented her with a potential mating pair.

She had been set up.

Jules ignored the tingling in her body, pushed aside her rising sexual tension and focused on her anger at being manipulated. Just as she was about to open her mouth and let them all know she wasn't going to play this game, her father called out to her, drawing her attention.

"Aren't you going to say hello, Jules?" Marcus may have asked her quietly, but it was still an order.

The expressions on her fathers' faces were not that of devoted parents but rather that of Leos determined to do their job and honor their Pride. She saw she had no choice but to play their game. For now.

"Gabe. Luke. It's been a long time," she choked out.

The corners of Gabe's mouth tilted up ever so slightly, the small smile playing around his lips making him more handsome than before. "Three years."

Those words, *three years*, said in such a mocking way brought a flush to her cheeks and moisture between the folds of her sex. Three years ago these men had stirred her body and those thoughts had been hovering in her mind ever since the mate call had gone out. Gabe was thinking along the same line; the heat in his eyes gave him away. A quick glance at Luke, and yeah, he was right there with them.

"I saw you in town two weeks ago, Luke. You never said Gabe was coming home for a visit." Jules held her breath waiting for his reply; maybe she was jumping to conclusions and this wasn't what it seemed. That hope was short lived when Luke spoke up.

"Gabe isn't home for a visit, Jules," he paused, letting the implication sink in. "He resigned his commission. Gabe is home to stay." What he didn't say was Gabe was home to stay with him. A pair of Lions, brothers, together.

"Good for Gabe." Not so good for her.

"Jules—" Dane barked in warning at her tone.

"What?" she snapped, looking at her father.

"You—" Dane started again but was cut off by his wife before he could go any further.

"Gentlemen, I did not spend hours cooking our meal to have it dry out and get cold before we could eat. Dane, Marcus, take our guests to the dining room please. Get them something to drink. Jules and I will follow in a minute with dinner." When no one made a move to follow her suggestion, Cherry picked up the salad bowl and pushed it into Luke's hands. "Luke, please take this to the table. There's a good bottle of merlot breathing on the table, waiting to be poured. Will you do the honors? Please," she added with a sigh when he didn't respond. "Jules and I will join you in a few minutes."

Luke finally took his gaze away from Jules' flushed face, looked down at her mother then nodded once. "I'd be happy to. Dane, it's been a long time since we've been here. Show us the way?"

After another tense moment of Dane shooting dark looks at both his wife and daughter, he nodded his agreement and led the men out of the kitchen.

Jules waited until her fathers and the Becketts headed down the hall then turned her fury on her mother. "You knew," she accused, her voice laced with both anger and hurt. "You weren't surprised to see Gabe. You knew he was back and you know what that means. Why didn't you tell me?" She felt betrayed by the lack of warning and let her mother know it.

"I knew," she agreed. "I didn't tell you because you wouldn't have come to dinner if you knew Gabe would be here. Jules, talk to them, get to know them. You haven't seen Gabe and Luke together or even been around them much since you were a child. They're good men, Jules. Give this a chance and see where it goes."

"They've already decided this, haven't they, Mom? They chose the Becketts, didn't they?" Jules didn't need the words, she saw the answer in her mother's eyes. "Damn them." And damn her for not realizing sooner something was up. She should have known this morning when her father cautiously asked if she wanted them to choose her mates for her. She felt betrayed. Hurt, angry and betrayed. But she wanted to hear it from her mother. She needed the truth. "When did they decide?"

"Jules, you know your fathers have a duty to the Pride. Part of the Leos' job is protecting the Pride. That includes naming their successors. Can you honestly tell me any of the Lions who have pursued you are up to the task? Isn't that part of the reason you've been so upset about the mate call? You know what it takes to lead the Pride and so far not one pair has been up to the job. Gabe and Luke are good men. They're smart and strong and can lead our people, Jules. They—"

Jules was not going to listen to a list of their virtues. "You didn't answer the question. When did they decide on the Becketts?"

"Three years ago."

Three years. The last time Gabe was home on leave. The shit she'd put up with the past months had been for nothing if her fathers had already made the decision. She was shocked by her mother's admission.

"They told your fathers three years ago they wanted to mate you, and your fathers agreed. You were still in school then, too young for a mating. Gabe and Luke wanted you to finish school, wanted to wait until you were older. There was no point in telling you then."

"Why did they make the announcement, the mate call? Why then, when Gabe was still in the Navy?" If her mating was a done deal why had her fathers gone through the pretense of letting her select her own mates?

"You were making noises about leaving the Pride. We could

see how restless you were. Others saw it too. So many of our young Lions have left to live outside the Pride, married with Non-Weres." Her smile was small and sad as she looked at her daughter. "Your fathers were afraid if you left you wouldn't come back. You are the next Lioness. It's an important role in our society, an honorable one. Our people expect you to mate the next Leos. It's our tradition, our way. If you left and didn't come back the future leadership of our people would be in jeopardy. You are such a strong woman, Jules. You're smart and tough. You will be a good Lioness, one our people can be proud of. Gabe needed time to settle his affairs with the Navy. Until he was back Luke had to keep quiet. The mate call went out as a way to keep you here and buy some time until they could claim you. We couldn't let you leave."

"So you lied. Yes you did, Mom," she growled when her mother shook her head in denial. "You should have told me the truth."

"If we had, what would you have done? You'd have left as fast as you could. You're stubborn, Jules. If we had told you Gabe and Luke would be your mates you'd have been angry the choice had been made for you and you'd have run. They are the best choice. You know that. The Pride will accept them. You will accept them."

Jules wouldn't say it but her mother was right. If presented as a done deal she would have run. The choice should have been hers. "What makes you think I want them as mates? That I would accept this?"

"Because you want them. You're attracted to them and have been for years."

"No I—"

"I could smell it. I can still smell it. Even though they're down the hall and out of sight the pull is still there."

Jules blushed. If her arousal was strong enough for her mother, a female Lion, to pick up, Jules knew Gabe and Luke, two Lions in their prime, had smelled it too. And her fathers. She was mortified. Everyone in the room had known she was attracted to them. "My body may want them but that doesn't mean *I* do."

"You don't want to be told what to do, Jules. WereLions are primal, sensual people. Our bodies often accept what our minds cannot. Your instincts are telling you to mate with these men. No other pair has affected you this way. When you calm down you'll realize I'm telling you the truth."

Calm down? Not likely. Her muscles ached from pent-up frustration and rage. She would give anything to be able to shift and run until she was too tired and sore to think or feel, until her paws ached from covering the hard ground, but she couldn't; female WereLions could shift only when in heat or gravely injured. She may not be able to shift and run but she could still drive and run. Getting away from this, from them, for a while so she could clear her head and deal with this was her only option.

"I can't deal with this now." She walked around her mother, heading for the door before she said something she would regret.

Cherry grabbed her arm before she made it over the threshold. "Sit down with them, with us and eat dinner, Jules. You can't walk away from this. Give Gabe and Luke a chance."

"Not now, Mom. I just...I can't right now." Something in the way she said that must have gotten through because Cherry dropped her arm and let her go.

"Where is she?" Gabe asked when Cherry came into the dining room alone a few minutes later.

"Cherry," Dane growled when she didn't answer.

"She went upstairs. She's not stupid, Dane. She saw this for what it is. I told you I didn't think this was a good idea, confronting her in her own home. Give her some time to get used to this—"

"She's had three months to get used to this, Cherry," Luke broke in, crossing his arms over his wide chest.

"To this, yes, but not to *you*. It was a mistake to let her know this way, for her to find out Gabe is back to stay. The mate call was a mistake. We should have been honest with her from the beginning. Jules knows her duty and she'll live up to it. The past three months have proved that. Her back is up now. She's angry and hurt. Give her some time."

"Gabe?" Luke arched his eyebrow in question.

"She'll run. Cover the front. I'll take the back."

"Gabriel—" Cherry protested.

"Does she know everything?"

"Yes, I told her."

"Why in hell would you do that?" Dane barked.

"Because she deserved to know, Dane," she barked right back. "It was the right thing to do."

"Cherry—" Marcus's voice was louder than she'd heard it in a long time.

But Luke cut him off before he could go on. "If she knows, there's no point in waiting," he reasoned. "Letting her run now will just make this harder. It's time for us to deal with her." Controlling their daughter was no longer the Leos' responsibility. That right belonged to her mates. When no one argued Luke knew her parents understood what he was saying.

The time had come.

They were going to claim their mate.

"Gabe, Luke," Marcus called to them as they were leaving the room. "She may be your mate but she's still our daughter. Remember that."

The brothers looked at their Leos, understood the warning. They'd been given permission to claim their mate and understood the responsibility that came with it. Jules came first. It was their responsibility to convince her to accept them as her mates. The brothers nodded once in acceptance of the warning then left.

Jules tossed her purse in the duffle, zipped it closed then sat on her bed and put on her running shoes. Short on time she only packed a few things, what she would need for the next day or so until she made it to her sister Nessa's place in Chicago. Santa Fe was too close to Logan, the Becketts, and to her family for her peace of mind so she'd scrapped her original plan, deciding instead to visit her sister; Nessa had a small apartment in Chicago where she was in law school. Jules knew her sister would put her up and not rat her out. In a few days she'd call her mother so she didn't worry; the only concession to her parents she was willing to make.

There were so many parts of this mess that made her angry she didn't know what to scream about first, but that would have to wait until she was on the road. Jules grabbed the duffle and slung her laptop case over her shoulder then opened the double French windows overlooking the back of the driveway and the pastures beyond. The last time she had snuck out of the house through this window was during her senior year in high school to meet a boyfriend her fathers had not thought highly of. It was ironic this trip out the window was to get away from two men her fathers expected her to get involved with.

Somehow she thought the irony would be lost on them.

A quick look out the window told her the coast was clear. For her sake she hoped all the people she was trying to get away from were still in the dining room, on the other side of the house. Jules dropped the duffle to the ground, and reached through the open window, latching on to the ivy trellis. It was only a twenty-foot drop, one her body could handle, but she opted to climb down halfway and not risk an injury she'd have to shift to heal.

She felt ridiculous sneaking out; she was twenty-three, not thirteen. She should be able to hold her head high and walk through the front door like an adult. And she would have if Gabe and Luke weren't downstairs. Seeing them again was a risk she wasn't willing to take. For so many, many reasons.

Hitching her computer case higher, Jules put one leg out the window, found a foothold on the trellis, then pulled the rest of her body through and started down. Midway between the window and the ground she let go and jumped.

Into the strong arms of one very pissed-off Lion.

Chapter Four

Luke heard them before he saw them and when they finally came into view he laughed as his brother came around the corner of the house, or rather limped around the corner of the house, with a very angry, very loud mate, ass end up over his shoulder.

"Put me down you rotten, no good—" Jules demanded, her words punctuated by the blows she rained over Gabe's back but cut short by the hard smack of his hand on her ass. "Ow! Damn you! You have no right—"

"I have every right, Jules. Settle down!" When she failed to comply he smacked her ass again, this time harder, which only made her fight him more. "Damn it, I said stop!" he yelled when her fist connected with his kidney; she was no match for a Lion in his prime but her blows packed enough punch to bruise. "That's enough. As soon as we get you home I'm going to paddle your bare ass until it's bright red if you don't stop acting like this."

"Home?" she screeched. "I'm not going home with you. I'm not going anywhere with you. Let me go!"

"Need some help, Gabe?" The smile in Luke's voice was as big as the one on his face.

"Take her bags," he grunted, tossing his brother her duffle and computer case. "What are you so damn happy about?"

"That she decided to sneak out the back instead of coming out the front." Luke caught the bags with one hand, reaching out to tug on Jules' hair hanging over his brother's ass with the other as Gabe came up next to him. Luke laughed again as Jules swatted blindly at him, letting out another screech. "If she had come my way I'd be the one limping, not you."

"Luke, make him put me down. He can't do this." Jules arched her neck, raising her head to look at Luke. She had always thought of him as the more reasonable brother and hoped to find help in his quarter. The smug smile creasing his handsome face had her back to cursing instead of asking for help. "This isn't right. I don't want to go with you."

"If I were you I'd listen to Gabe and calm down."

"What is it going to take to get you jerks to understand that I don't want you? I am not going to mate with you."

"You're already our mate, Jules. Once we get you back to the ranch and claim you, you'll understand that." This edict came from Gabe as he yanked open the passenger door of their pick-up truck.

Claiming? Back to their ranch? No. No, no, no. "There is no way I'm going to your ranch with you so you two can fuck me. I decide who I fuck and you can damn well bank on it not being you two."

Smack, another hard swat on her ass from Gabe before he lifted her off his shoulder and pushed her into the truck. "Don't talk like that, Jules. That kind of language doesn't suit you."

"How do you know what suits me or not? You don't *know* me." In the truck she was pulled onto Gabe's lap, his arms wrapped around her, keeping her hands trapped from doing any damage. She ignored the dark look Luke sent her way as he got behind the wheel. Neither one of these men were listening. "My parents will not put up with you taking me." She hoped that was true but their complete lack of concern cut that line of reasoning short.

"Your fathers know we're taking you to the Roaring Lion. This is a done deal, Jules. Start accepting it." Luke started the truck then headed down the long drive to the main road. "Your body already has, Jules. Open your mind to what your body already knows and this will be easier for you."

The casual mention of her attraction and resulting arousal to the brothers filled the truck cab like humidity filled the late summer air, making it hard to breathe and her body uncomfortably warm. Gabe's erection pressing into the curve of her ass showed her she wasn't the only one affected by Luke's comments. The fight didn't go out of her, instead it shifted from thoughts of escaping these two to controlling her reaction to them.

"Don't flatter yourself. *Yourselves.* What you think is attraction to you is nothing more than my having a normal, healthy sex drive."

"How many other pairs have you let know about your *healthy sex drive*?"

Jules snapped her mouth closed. That was the whole problem, why these two worried her more than all the others combined. No other pair affected her the way Gabe and Luke did. If she thought she could get away with it Jules would have lied through her teeth, claimed she'd had a similar reaction to another man or men, but she didn't. She kept her mouth shut. If she wasn't able to believe the lie how would they?

The remainder of the short ride to the Roaring Lion was completed in silence. No one was talking but that didn't mean nothing was going on. Jules sat stiffly on Gabe's lap, trying her damnedest but failing miserably at ignoring his hard-on. The sexual tension inside the cab was stifling. The Beckett brothers were determined to take what they wanted and Jules was silently scrambling to think of a way to stop it.

Luke parked the truck on the side of the house near the kitchen door. Jules didn't take the time to admire the changes they had made to the stately three-story main house since the last time she'd been here. Outside the truck, Gabe kept a firm hold on her, not taking a chance on her running. She shook with frustration. What was it going to take to make them understand she didn't want this? When Gabe tugged on her arm, urging her to walk with him to the house, Jules dug in her heels, refusing to move. The brothers exchanged amused glances over her stubbornness.

"You can walk in the house with us like a grown woman or I can carry you in over my shoulder. But, Jules..." Gabe lifted her chin with one finger, bringing her eyes up to meet his, "...having your ass so handy to spank if you don't behave might be more temptation than I can resist."

The sexy glint in Gabe's eye told her just how appealing that thought was to him. And damn her if the thought of him doing just that didn't make her wet. Jules jerked her head away from his hand, shot Luke a fuming look telling him she didn't appreciate his amusement and headed for the house, leaving Gabe no choice but to let go of her arm or walk with her.

Inside, Luke tossed his keys on the table and set her bags on a chair. "Are you hungry?" He opened the refrigerator and peered inside.

"No." She was but she was too wired to eat. Jules watched as Luke pulled out three beers and several containers of leftovers while Gabe got down plates. How could they want to eat now? Wasn't that just like a man? They either thought with their stomachs or their dicks. There was too much for them to settle to take the time for dinner. "Why did you bring me here?"

Luke came toward her, offering her a beer. "This is your home now, Jules. We brought you home." He said it so simply, so straightforward, there was no doubt he believed what he was saying.

When Luke walked back to the counter to make himself a plate, Jules calculated her chances of swiping their keys, making it out the door and to the truck before they could catch her. With the guys' longer legs, stronger muscles and determination to get their own way, the odds were not in her favor. She watched them put together a meal, declining again when they asked her if she wanted to eat, completely dumbfounded by what they were doing.

She slammed the beer bottle she forgot she was holding onto the table with enough force to get both their attention. Enough was enough. "What can I say to make you understand I don't want this? I don't live here, Luke, this isn't my home." She picked up on his last remark. "We need to talk about this."

"We will. There's a lot we need to talk about, but not now. Tomorrow is soon enough to discuss our mating."

"Tomorrow?" What was he thinking? "We're not putting this off until tomorrow. Let's talk about this now, tonight." The sooner they understood she was not a willing participant, the sooner she could get the hell out of here and away from this mess and them.

"We have other things to do tonight, Jules." Gabe and Luke came up to the table. "More important things."

"What other things?" Her gaze darted between the two men. The two aroused men. By the look on their faces and the bulges in their pants it wasn't hard to figure out how they planned to spend the remainder of the evening. "If you think you brought me here to sleep with you, you're both crazy. I am *not* going to have sex with you!"

"This is more than us wanting to have sex with you, Jules." Gabe moved closer, almost close enough to touch her. "Once we've had each other you'll understand that we, the three of us, belong together."

She couldn't believe what she was hearing. "This..." she waved her hand between them, "...this can't be settled with sex. This is my life, Gabe. Don't you think I should have a say in who I mate with?"

"Are you telling us you want to mate with another pair?" Luke asked her.

"I don't want to mate with anybody. Not now."

"So there isn't anyone else?"

He was missing the point. "Listen to me. My finding mates, that was my fathers' idea. They want to step down and put me in a position I don't want to be in. Now you two think you're going to mate me—"

"We are your mates," Gabe growled.

"—and take over the Pride. Just because my fathers approve of you doesn't mean I have to go along with it."

Luke spoke up as Gabe growled again. "Does that mean you're going to step aside, leave the Pride and abandon your duty?"

"I never said that. I know what my duty is, Luke. But I don't like how I've been manipulated. When I become Lioness it will be when I'm ready. My mates will be men I choose."

"That's not how it's going to be." Gabe paced his words as if talking to a child. "The decision has been made, Jules. It was made three years ago. You weren't ready then but you are now, no matter what you think. The Leos agreed. It's your responsibility to do what's in the best interest of the Pride and part of that is accepting us as your mates."

"So you mate me and you get the Pride?" Jules knew that wasn't what Gabe meant but she said it anyway. She'd rather have two pissed-off Lions to deal with than two horny ones.

"Damn it, Jules!" Luke yelled.

"What? It's an honest question. Maybe a woman wants to know that she's wanted for herself rather than for what she brings to the table. You have to admit the reins of the Pride are a dowry not many Lions could resist."

"I'm only going to say this once, Jules, so listen up. Even if the Pride wasn't 'on the table' as you put it, we would still want you for our mate. We've known that for years. If you took the time to listen to your inner Lion you'd admit you want us as much as we want you. As much as we'd like the Pride to be a separate issue it isn't, and there's nothing we can do about that. Who you mate will be the Leos. That is a life-altering position we're willing to take on because we want *you*."

Jules could tell Gabe was angry, not by what he said and how he said it but by the look on his face. Luke was just as angry though he had kept quiet. She wasn't willing to give in to what they wanted. "If I wasn't the first born daughter of the Leos you'd still want to mate me? Both of you?"

When they nodded, Jules was shocked. These men really didn't know her. Why did they want her so badly? Then she had another thought. "Why would you two be willing to share a woman? Why not find your own mates?"

Leos always mated two to one. She'd heard of a few other Pride matings between triads rather than couples but those were rare.

"You've known for years you would have two mates. Can you tell me, and be honest with your answer, Jules," Luke cautioned, "that the idea of having two men in your bed didn't turn you on?"

Jules squirmed at the way he looked at her, like he already knew the truth. The *last* thing she would tell him or his brother was the truth. "This isn't about me, Luke. I'm asking about you and Gabe. Why would you want to share a woman?"

"It's natural for us."

"Don't blame this on your DNA. Most members of the Pride enter into monogamous relationships. My lineage is forcing me to accept two mates, yours isn't. Why should I think you two are any different from the other Lions who've been chasing my tail? So far all I've seen is pairs wanting to get their rocks off by going two on one. I've heard it all, every smarmy line a guy can come up with to convince me two in my bed would be better than one. Double the pleasure, double the fun. I think most of them pursued me for the kink factor alone." She shot both Gabe and Luke a look heavily doused with cynicism. "Is that how it is for you two? Is that how you get off?"

"It can be," Gabe answered honestly. "It has been in the past when we've shared women. But in this case, what's between us, it's more than just the kink. It's meant to be."

"Doesn't it bother you at all?" She shot both of them a disgusted look. "Knowing I'll be sleeping with both of you? That I'll get sweaty and hot with one of you then turn to the other for more of the same?" She'd intended to turn them off the idea of sharing her but what she said had the opposite effect. Interested desire darkened both their features.

"Sometimes it would be like that." Luke's voice, heavy and laced with need, sent a shiver down her spine. "One of us watching while the other fucked you, hard and ready and drinking in your cries while waiting for his turn. Other times you'd take us both, at the same time. One of us in your mouth while the other fucks your pussy, maybe one of us in your pussy and the other in your ass. There'll be times when we make love to you alone." Luke cupped her jaw, brushed his thumb over the fullness of her bottom lip. "I promise you'll be satisfied every way we take you."

Chapter Five

Heat flooded her sex at the pictures he painted of the three of them together. Just like in her dreams she saw them over her, on her, pleasuring her until she screamed for more. It was a reaction she couldn't keep private.

The brothers took a deep breath, drawing in the scent of her arousal. Jules gasped as they moved on her, Luke pressing into her front, Gabe taking up the rear, moving in tight against her back. They surrounded her. Their heat, their smell, their hands, they were all over her.

And damn her if that didn't turn her on.

It was wrong, she knew she should resist, but Jules stood frozen as they touched her. From behind, Gabe reached his arms around her and pulled her shirt from her pants then slid his hands underneath, moving them up her body to cup her breasts.

Jules watched Luke as he watched Gabe pull up her shirt and push her bra out of the way until her breasts were bare and available. But watching wasn't enough for Luke. Lowering his head, he flicked out his tongue to taste the pearled nipple of the breast his brother held plumped in his hand. Jules closed her eyes at the contact then released a breathy little moan when Luke took her nipple in his mouth. Her pussy throbbed in reaction to the pull and tug of his lips at her breast. Gabe cupped her other breast and worked the tip with his fingers, giving her more pleasure.

But soon they all needed more. Her arms, trapped as they were under Gabe's, were of no use in stopping Luke as he opened her jeans and pushed them and her panties to the floor. He had her shoes off and she was naked from the waist down before the protest left her lips.

"Damn, she's waxed, Gabe." Luke slipped two fingers between her legs to part her sex. "Smooth as silk. And she's wet. I wonder how she'll taste."

Luke pulled a chair out from the table, sat, then parted her legs far enough to make room for his mouth. She cried out as his lips found her moist core. Jules dropped her head onto Gabe's shoulder as Luke ate at her pussy. His tongue, his lips, he used them both to spread her lips and suck the pink flesh between. Then he licked her from the opening of her sex to the tip of her clit. Her legs trembled as she stood on her toes and angled her hips toward him.

Gabe felt the tremors in her body as he held her while his brother tasted what he could smell. Her scent had turned him on before, but now, here in the kitchen while his brother fucked her with his tongue, it drove him crazy. He ground his cock into the ass that had tempted in the truck, wishing he was naked. He needed to be inside her so bad he was about to burst, but he had to wait. This was for Jules. "How does she taste?" he ground out through clenched teeth as he palmed her breasts.

Luke lifted his head. "Like cotton candy. I've never tasted anything as sweet as Jules."

Gabe watched Luke lower his head, push inside her and fuck her with his tongue. When she took hold of his brother's head, running her fingers through his mane, and pressed him deeper into her sex, Gabe knew Luke was giving her what she was asking for.

"How does it feel, Jules?" Gabe needed to hear her say it.

"Good," she moaned. "So very, very good."

"Do you want more?"

"Yes."

"Tell him and he'll give it to you."

"I want to come," she cried as Luke tilted her hips forward and sank inside her again.

"Then you will."

And she did.

Gabe carried her through the bedroom door while Luke turned on the light and closed then locked the door behind them. Still reeling from her climax, Jules felt fuzzy and awkward when he set her on her feet. Her shirt and bra were still bunched up above her breasts but she was naked from the waist down. Embarrassed, she tugged at her clothes but didn't get far before two pairs of hands stopped her, stripped the shirt and bra from her body, leaving her naked. Jules didn't try to run or hide. She wanted this.

She watched as they stripped. Her mouth watered as they bared their chests and revealed their cocks. Clothed they were impressive, naked they were magnificent. They could have been twins, they looked so much alike. Wide shoulders, muscled chests, chiseled abs, lean hips, long strong legs; these men were eye candy. They were also well hung. Jules shivered in delight at the prospect of taking their thick, heavily veined, long cocks into her body. She didn't realize she was staring until she heard Gabe's amused chuckle.

"Like what you see?"

"Yes." She loved it. And she loved the way he stroked

himself from the thick base to the swollen crest. She almost came again right there and right then.

Naked and aroused, his sex jutting proudly from the nest of dark brown curls at his groin, Luke backed her to the bed, picked her up and laid her down in the middle. He took his place beside her as Gabe joined them, one Lion on each side.

Then they started.

Hands and lips touched her everywhere. Jules closed her eyes as they roamed over her body. She didn't know whose lips were sucking her nipples or whose hand was parting her sex. And she didn't care. They took turns kissing her and stroking her. These men had no shame.

Being the center of their attention would be enough for some women but it wasn't enough for Jules. She wanted to be an active participant. She laughed as they groaned when she took a cock in each hand. Silk-covered steel, that's what they felt like.

Luke stopped kissing her neck to rest his head on her shoulder as she palmed his sex. "Harder." He moved his hips, sliding his erection through her hand. She fisted their cocks then rubbed her thumbs over the heads, pressing on their slits and spreading the drops of fluid that pearled on top. Encouraged by their mutual sounds of satisfaction, Jules stroked the spots just under the heads, the place she knew would drive them wild. When they pulled away she let out a moan. She was disappointed. She wanted to play.

Gabe moved between her legs, sat back on his heels and pulled her thighs over his, leaving her wide open and vulnerable while Luke moved to the top of the bed behind her and took her hands in his, stretching her arms over her head. Her belly quivered, part in fear, part in anticipation, at the way they held her down. Like this, prone between the two of them, they could do anything they wanted. Jules wished they would.

Gabe needed to touch her, to put his hands on her and make her understand who she belonged to. He started with the smooth mound above her sex, running his fingers over the bare skin. He loved the look of a waxed pussy but he loved the delicate pink flesh between the bare lips even more. Parting her, he looked his fill. Her swollen clit stood out, demanding his attention. Did she like it hard or did she prefer a gentle touch? He wanted to know everything that turned this woman on. Gabe started slowly, rubbing her gently then applied more pressure to the sensitive nub as she pressed her sex into his palm, asking for more. Moisture leaked from the tiny opening of her vagina as her body reacted to his touch. Still holding her lips open, Gabe pushed two fingers inside her.

"She's so tight," he told Luke as he fingered her. If she felt this good around his fingers what would she feel like around his cock? Gabe pulled out and licked her sweet cream from his fingers. "You're right. Just like cotton candy." He reached up and stroked Jules' lips with his wet fingers. "Open up and see how good you taste." He cursed when she did.

Gabe shot his brother a heated look, telling him it was time. While Luke bent low and took her lips, Gabe positioned his sex at the opening of hers and pushed forward just enough for the head to pass through. He felt her tense and watched as she jerked her lips from Luke's, ready to stop him.

"You can do this, baby," Luke whispered against her lips, holding her head still. He stroked her hair off her face and held her tight. "Relax and let him in."

She wasn't a virgin but she was tight. Gabe flexed his hips and pressed deeper until half his cock was gripped inside her, then stopped, giving her a moment to adjust before moving again and sliding home. Heat, warmth, cream, he felt it all through the nerves of his cock. It was the best feeling he'd ever had.

She'd only had two lovers and neither of them had been as big as Gabe. Her muscles burned as they stretched to accommodate his girth. Jules closed her eyes as Luke stroked her hair, encouraging her to relax. Just when she thought she could stand the pressure Gabe moved, rasping her tender insides as he stretched her further, wider. Steadily, Gabe increased his thrusts as he plowed through her resistance and broke it down.

She never saw Luke move but was thankful that he did as he rubbed her clit. The intense pleasure his hand gave her eased the pain of Gabe's penetration. Heat flushed her cells as the two of them played with her sex. Pleasure coiled in her pelvis as the pressure of their combined efforts built inside her, nudging her closer to a climax. Gabe pumped faster as she writhed on the bed.

"That's it, Jules. Take it from him, baby." Luke grunted with approval as she lifted her hips into Gabe's thrusts. He tickled her clit twice then watched as she came. Jules closed her eyes as she gave over to her orgasm.

But they weren't done with her, not yet. Gabe continued to shaft her pussy as Luke moved to her head, settled on his side and pressed his hungry cock to her lips. She licked the head then the shaft, running her tongue over the vein marking the underside of his long length before taking him between her lips and sucking him deep to the back of her throat. Jules moaned around Luke's shaft as Gabe shifted to his knees, placed her legs around his waist and fucked her harder. She didn't know what was better: Luke in her mouth or Gabe in her cunt. Sensing they were close to coming, Jules sucked Luke harder while she tightened on Gabe's cock as she teetered on the edge of release again. All three came together. The men moaned as they filled her with their semen and she groaned as she took what they had to give.

Spent and sated, they pulled out from her body then came down beside her, Luke on her right, Gabe on her left, and tucked her close.

Chapter Six

Jules opened her eyes to the morning sunshine streaming through the bare windows. She blinked a few times, adjusting to the brightness before rolling to her back, then shut her eyes again, this time to the memories of what happened last night. Her fantasies had never come close to the reality of Gabe and Luke making love to her. She ached pleasantly in all the right places. She was torn between falling back asleep to relive their loving in her dreams and finding a way to escape them so she had peace and solitude to think about what she was going to do.

Last night spent in their bed had made her situation worse, not better. If she gave in and accepted their claiming, Jules was afraid it would set the tone for the rest of their lives; her acquiescing to their demands. Even though Gabe and Luke had spent hours loving her body, it was still just a night of hot sex. Could they exist the rest of their lives together with sexual attraction being their only bond? The sex between them had been hot but giving in to the demands of her body clouded the issue of their situation and nothing more. No matter what they'd experienced together, she still had a problem with this mating being forced on her and the worry that she wasn't ready for this kind of lifetime commitment. Jules needed to think it all through and what her inability to resist them meant, but she was just too tired to deal with such heavy thoughts.

"It's too early for you to be thinking so hard."

Any lingering feeling of sleepiness slid away as Jules realized she was not alone. She turned her head to the right and the sound of Gabe's voice. He was lying on his side, his head propped up on one hand. The sheet over him came up to just under his hips, covering his groin and legs but exposing the trident tattoo low on the inner curve of his right hip. Last night she had thought it was sexy, this morning she still did. Though she was covered, Jules tucked her portion of the sheet tighter under her arms. Gabe smiled at her but didn't comment, which had her feeling all the more foolish. Modesty had no place rearing its head after what took place in this bed last night.

"What time is it?"

"A little after ten. I was beginning to think you were going to sleep the day away."

"Where's Luke?"

"Working in the west pasture replacing fencing. He left around six this morning."

"Did you stay to keep an eye on me?"

"Yes." The smile in his voice reflected in his eyes.

"At least you're honest." If Gabe stayed that meant they thought she'd run if given the chance. *Smart men.*

"I'll never lie to you, Jules. Neither will Luke."

"You already did."

Gabe understood what she meant. "You think by not telling you sooner we would be your mates, we lied," he stated. "When should we have told you, Jules? When the decision was made years ago? If we had, you would have been fighting this for three years. Instead you finished school without that weighing on your mind. If you'd found out the truth three months ago you would have still tried to run. Luke and I don't care for what's gone on since your fathers made the announcement, but overall you finding out last night, that was the best way to handle it."

"My mating could have waited a few years. I accept my responsibility to the Pride, Gabe. I will be the next Lioness. Your plans were cut short by my fathers' announcement just like mine were. How did you feel about having to leave the Navy?"

Gabe reached out to play with a curl of her hair as he thought about his answer. "I was in the Navy a long time, was a Seal for the last seven years. A while back, maybe five, six years ago, I thought I'd make a career of it; stay in for my twenty then retire. It's not because I didn't like the ranch. This is my home and always will be, but being part of the teams and the work we did appealed to me, both sides of me; man and Lion. You'd be surprised how many Weres are in the service. Not just Lions but Wolves and Tigers too. Protecting and defending comes naturally to us. I knew Luke was planning on coming back to the Roaring Lion after college and the ranch would be in good hands. His coming back here gave me the opportunity to serve my country and my people." Gabe spoke evenly, almost quietly, but he wanted her to see his time in the Navy had been important to him, an important part of him.

"If it meant so much to you why did you resign?"

He smiled down at her, his fingers still playing with her hair. "This is home. This is my Pride. This is where you are."

"You resigned because of me? Gabe, we hardly know each other. Yeah, I knew you when I was a kid but that was years ago and back then you were more likely to snarl at me than smile. We're practically strangers. I don't understand why you'd give up your career for me."

He could tell she really didn't understand what he was

saying. "You know, I've seen friends, my human friends and teammates, go through woman after woman trying to find the one meant for them. I've listened to them talk, wondering about how they'd know when they found the right woman, the one they'd want to spend the rest of their lives with. As a Were, I knew I'd never have that problem. When the right woman came along I'd know. And I did. So did Luke. We knew you were the right one for us when we saw you the last time I was home on leave."

"The scent thing," she muttered. "What is it with you guys and the sniffing?"

"Who's been sniffing you?" he growled.

"Who hasn't?" she shot back. "You have no idea what I've gone through since the mate call went out. Every Lion who wants to be Leo has been sniffing around me. You guys have no respect for personal space."

His muscles flexed as his possessive instincts roared at the mention of other Lions and their interest in his mate. Through a combined effort of his training as a SEAL and the control he had mastered as a Lion, Gabe tamped down the urge to demand she stay away from other males. If he thought for a moment she was interested in another pair he would have ordered her to stay away from them, might have locked her up so they couldn't get to her, but he knew that wasn't the case. If she was interested in any of the others who had sought her out she would never have responded to him and Luke like she had.

"You don't have to worry about that anymore." The words came out harsher than he liked but he didn't take them back or make any excuses. "But, yeah. You could call it the scent thing. And don't think I didn't notice you before that. You were maybe seventeen, eighteen the first time I saw you as something other than my kid sister's friend. That's how it starts for us. When you were twenty and I saw you for the first time as an adult, I knew. You had the sweetest smell I'd ever encountered, like jasmine on the air of a warm summer night. Luke felt the same way. Can you deny you didn't feel the same kind of pull?" When she didn't answer right away Gabe knew he was right; she couldn't deny it and that was part of the problem. His mate was just too stubborn to admit it.

"How do I know this…this…" she waved her hand, "…attraction is nothing more than a healthy sex drive that needs some action?"

He edged closer to her then flicked his wrist, pulling the sheet, discarding it at the end of the bed, leaving them both naked. Before she could move away, he pressed one hand between her legs to cup her sex. His cock twitched as her moist warmth filled his palm. Gabe grunted in approval as her thighs spread ever so slightly, making room for his hand; she wanted his hands on her. The full, rounded globes of her breasts were too much for him to resist. Lowering his head, he blew softly over the tip of her left breast before stroking it with his tongue.

"Don't discount this, sweetheart. You don't respond to others like you do to Luke and me," he whispered against her puckered nipple. "When we mate, we mate for life. Our senses, our bodies tell us when we've found the right mate." He eased two fingers into her pussy, pushing past the tight resistance at the same moment his mouth claimed her nipple. Rhythmically, he sucked and fucked her, working her body with his hand and mouth until she arched into him, begging for more. His hair was still military short but there was enough of it for her to thread her fingers through the dark blond strands. Her hold on him tight, she pressed him deeper into her breast, silently asking for more.

He was happy to oblige. Moving from one to the other, he loved her breasts with his mouth. Nips, kisses, licks, bites, he ate at her like he was a starving man and she was a feast prepared just for him. But he needed more. Keeping up the rhythm between her legs, he fucked her with his fingers like he owned her, his chest swelling like his cock with pride each time her inner muscles contracted in need around him. The sweet scent of her sex and desire filled the air. She wanted him. And he wanted more.

Like a man on a mission, Gabe moved over her and kissed his way down her body to the bare skin above her sex. Spreading her thighs he settled between them, slid his hands under her ass and lifted her to his mouth. One long sweep of his tongue through her moist slit had her begging for more. He gave her what she needed. Over and over he licked her, lapping up her sweet juice. Spreading her legs wider, opening for him, she was rewarded when his tongue delved inside her.

He had never tasted anything as sweet as Jules in the morning. His mouth buried in her sex, he fucked her with his tongue like he had the night before with his cock.

"Don't stop, Gabe. Please, please, don't stop," she begged. "Gabe..."

He raised his head just enough to look up her body, pleased to see her arching off the bed, her fisted hands twisting the sheets. She was so close. Just a little more and she'd go over. His woman wanted him. "You want more?"

"God, yes..."

He was ready to give it to her. But when she came she would come with him. Gabe rose to his knees, leaned over her and kissed her, cutting off her cry of disappointment with his lips still wet from her pussy. "Turn over," he ordered, lifting his head. "Roll over, get on your hands and knees." Gabe knelt behind her and watched with a hungry gaze as she turned, as her ass lifted in the air, the lips of her wet sex peeking through the slight part of her thighs. His cock bobbed, straining toward his belly; he needed to be inside her so bad he was about to burst but he needed something else more. "Open for me. Spread your legs wide so I can see you."

"Gabe...Gabe, please..."

He didn't realize he was holding his breath until it burst from his lungs. This was how he wanted her; ready and willing to accept him. He had waited three years for this. In the wild, lions mounted their mates and in this bed, their bed, he mounted his. Gabe covered her with his body. One hand held her still, while the other guided his shaft to her small opening and he pushed into her tight sheath until he was buried to the hilt. Instinct took over as he rode her hard, pushing deep with each thrust. Nothing had ever felt as good as being inside her body.

"I'll give you what you want as soon as you give me what I want, Jules. Open for me."

Jules turned her head, looking over her shoulder so she could see him. Naked, on his knees, he looked so imposing, his wide chest roped with muscles damp with a light sheen of sweat. His cock was as long and thick as she remembered from last night. What he'd done to her last night she wanted to experience again. She knew what he wanted. Last night they had maneuvered her into accepting them in her bed. Today, he wanted her to give herself over to him freely, with no hesitation or reservations. She could hear it in his voice. She may not agree she was his mate, but he needed her to submit to him and she...damn her...but she needed to give over to what he needed.

"Jules..."

He didn't plead, he didn't beg but she sensed it, the need he had. She saw it on his face and in the tight, straight line of his shoulders. She wanted the release, the passion, and he wanted something in return. Not looking too closely at why she was doing it, Jules eased her legs apart. She felt exposed, like this, open for him to look at. It was scary and exhilarating at the same time.

"Wider," he grunted then rewarded her with a gentle caress on her ass as she slid her knees wider on the bed, showing him everything she had. When he reached forward and placed his hand between her shoulders she knew what he wanted and leaned forward until her shoulders hit the mattress.

This was the ultimate position of submission.

Jules moved with him, accepting his thrusts. Every nerve in her body felt like it was alive. Just when she thought she couldn't take any more he slowed down, backed off, denying her the climax that hovered inside her. She cursed him, then cursed him again when he laughed. He was playing with her and she didn't like it. On his next thrust she tightened around him, clamping down on his cock. This time she was the one who laughed when he cursed. The laughter didn't last long as his finger stroked her clit, driving her wild and she begged him for more.

When he gave her what she needed she returned the favor, urging him to finish them both. One finger on her clit drove her wild while he plowed her with his cock. A few strokes later he rammed inside her, pushing her forward as he leaned over her body and gave her his semen, flooding her cunt with everything he had. When he was spent, Gabe collapsed on top of her, taking her down to the mattress then rolled to his side, still buried inside her. He pulled her close and licked the sweat from her throat and neck as she shook with the aftershocks of their climax. She didn't want him to pull out, to leave her. Jules wanted to stay like this forever, wanted him inside her, a part of her. And feeling like that, it scared the hell out of her.

They made it downstairs just after one in the afternoon. Luke joined them for lunch a few minutes later. Jules felt awkward being with the two of them in the same room after spending the morning in bed with Gabe. Last night it had been easy being with both of them. It had been easy being with just Gabe. Jules didn't want to know what that said about her, how casually she'd lain with both of them. WereLions were open about sex but not this open. It crossed her mind more than once as she helped them make lunch what Luke would think about her and Gabe having sex while he was working. It turned out she didn't have anything to worry about.

"Did Gabe take care of you this morning?" He hugged her from behind while she was setting the table. He chuckled in her ear when she dropped a plate. "There's nothing to be embarrassed about, Jules. Once Gabe is settled on the ranch I'll be the one sleeping in and taking care of you in the mornings."

"You wish," Gabe threw out. "We started a routine this morning. You think I'm going to give that up?"

"Don't you think," Jules said, trying to shrug out of Luke's hold, "that both of you are taking a lot for granted."

"No," they answered at the same time.

Wasn't that just like a man...men. "Well, I do."

"You think too much." Luke kissed her jaw before letting her go.

"You say that like it's a bad thing."

"It is." Again they answered together.

Jules snapped her teeth as she turned on them. "Do you two ever have an independent thought?"

"You should be happy we're so much alike, Jules." Gabe set

a platter of sandwiches on the table then pulled out a chair and sat. "It'll make your life easier."

There was nothing easy about these two. "Again with the assumptions. Last night you put a stop to our discussion but that doesn't mean it's over. We need to talk about this like adults."

Luke brought a pitcher of sweet tea and glasses to the table then took his seat. "I thought we settled this last night."

"Nothing was settled."

"We claimed you, Jules."

"We had sex, Gabe," she countered. "Don't read more into it than that." She took her own seat and filled her plate. "Just because I slept with you doesn't mean I've changed my mind." She looked at both of them as she took a sip of her tea. "After lunch I want you to take me back to the Double K." She'd expected an argument or at least an outright refusal of her request. When neither of them said anything she thought they might not have heard her. "I need to get back home. I have things to do today." Again, no reaction. Jules sat back and watched them devour their sandwiches. "You're ignoring me, aren't you?"

"Yes."

"Knock off the tandem answers. I need to go home."

"You mean you need to leave," Luke corrected. "Don't forget those clean clothes you're wearing today came from the bag you packed and threw out your window last night. You were planning on running, Jules."

"There is no more running. I thought we settled that this morning when we talked."

"We talked for five minutes then stopped to have sex, Gabe. Nothing was settled." What did she have to say to get through to them? "I need you two to listen to me and hear what I'm saying."

Gabe set down his sandwich. "Look, you didn't eat anything last night and we skipped breakfast this morning. Have something to eat then later we'll talk. You know what's going on between us is more important than just what you want. We say we claimed you, you say we didn't. That isn't going to change over lunch. Spend the day with us and see what happens."

His request was reasonable. He wasn't being demanding or asking her for something outrageous. If anything, Jules thought he was being sincere. "Okay—" she picked up her sandwich, "—but no more sex." She could think straight if they kept their hands off her.

"Yeah, right." Gabe and Luke may have said it together but she thought it at the same time.

Chapter Seven

Like the day before, Jules woke to find Gabe in bed with her, not watching her like yesterday but wrapped around her, holding her close, one hand cupping a breast, the other buried between her legs. Even in sleep he wasn't letting her go.

Yesterday she'd spent the day with them like Gabe had asked. She never argued or tried to convince them to take her home. Not that there was any chance they were going to. These Lions were determined to keep her right where she was until she accepted their claim and they were willing to do whatever they could to keep her mind off leaving. To them that meant sex, sex, and more sex. After spending a few hours touring the main compound of the ranch, Luke had suggested taking a break and getting something to drink. They weren't back in the house for more than ten minutes before the three of them were naked in the great room, testing the springs of the couch.

Dinner was made and eaten with her dressed only in Luke's shirt, which provided him and Gabe easy access to pet and caress her whenever she was in reach. They had dessert in bed. If the Pride gave out awards for sexual stamina, the Becketts would have a wall of blue ribbons. How did they expect her to think when she was in a constant state of arousal? They didn't, that's how. They wanted her open and ready for their touch, not thinking of ways to talk them out of a mating.

She had to give them points for creativity. Nothing was taboo to these men. They took her as a pair, individually, had even coaxed her into pleasuring herself while they watched. Watching them take their cocks in their own hands was a sight she would never forget. She grew warm and wet remembering what she'd done with them.

"Happy thoughts?" Gabe purred in her ear, letting her know he was awake. "Make that *wet*, happy thoughts," he said as the hand between her legs parted her sex and two fingers slid inside.

"No more, Gabe," she protested even as she moved her hips, asking for more.

"Yes more."

"Didn't you get enough last night?"

"I can never get enough of you."

His thumb found her clit and pressed down. Damn, he was good. But she had to be better. "We can't spend the morning in bed. We have to—"

"You're right. We have to. If you don't want to do it in bed let's try the shower." Gabe jumped out of bed and hauled her up in his arms so fast her head spun.

It was a hell of a way to start the day.

Even though it was Sunday it was not a day of rest for the crew at the Roaring Lion. Everyone who worked at the ranch got two days off a week but not always on a weekend. Luke was at the stables working with the vet and Gabe needed to spend some time reacquainting himself with the ranch and the changes his brother had made since taking over. They still weren't letting her out of their sight longer than it took to take a shower or use the bathroom so she had no choice but to get in the truck and go with Gabe to look over different parts of their operation. Before she knew it, the morning was gone and it was time for lunch.

"Do you remember Raging Black?" Gabe asked as they drove back to the main compound of the ranch.

"Your stallion?" Raging Black was a beautiful, powerful horse, one of the studs on the ranch.

"Yeah. Summer's Rain dropped his colt a few weeks back. How about we stop by the stable and take a look before going in for lunch? Luke said he's not as skittish around people anymore. I'd like to take a look at him."

Jules agreed. The rest of the ride to the stables passed with conversation on the Roaring Lion's horse breeding operation. Gabe told her how Luke was responsible for growing that side of their business, making it as profitable as their cattle ranching. It was easy to see how proud he was of his brother's accomplishments.

When they reached the stables, they went in and found Luke talking with the staff vet. He made introductions then steered the conversation back to what they'd been discussing, bringing Gabe up to speed. Jules listened for a few minutes then left them to their work. Strolling down the main aisle she peeked into stalls, stopped to pet a few of the horses. She'd grown up around horses and was familiar with the sights, sounds and smells of a stable. She was impressed by what she saw. The Becketts ran a first-class operation.

Twenty minutes later the brothers found her, one foot propped on the door of a stall, petting the horse standing docile inside. "That's Starlight." Luke came up next to her and held out a hand to the mare. "She's one of the horses we keep on the ranch for pleasure riding. Jenna rides her when she visits. She'll be a good mount for you."

Jules bristled at the implication that her being here permanently was a foregone conclusion. This wasn't the first time he or Gabe had made such statements or casual references to her future over the past few days. She didn't bother correcting Luke's assumption this time; every other time she'd spoken up, one or both of the men ignored what she had to say as if she'd never said a word.

"Done with the vet?" she asked, changing the subject.

"For now. Gabe and I will meet with him again tomorrow."

"Let's take a look at the colt." Gabe took her hand, pulling her from the stall. "Have you decided on a name, Luke?"

"Not yet. I want to get to know him a bit more." His answer made Jules smile. She'd always thought it was sweet the way he personally named the horses born on the ranch.

"Are you keeping the colt or will you sell him?" They stopped at another stall and Jules looked in.

"Keep him. Raging Black was a great horse; he still is. I think his son will be the same." Luke extended a hand over the half door of the stall. "Aren't you boy," he whispered softly as the spindly colt came up to sniff his hand.

"He's beautiful," Jules whispered as they watched the colt. After a few minutes the animal relaxed enough to approach Jules and Gabe. The three of them talked softly as they watched the colt, smiling over his antics.

The radio on Luke's belt beeped before a tinny voice came over the speaker. "Luke, you there?"

Luke plucked the radio from his belt. "What do you need?"

"The men are ready to head out to the east pasture. How many head do you want moved?"

"Tell him I'll come out." Gabe moved closer to Jules, tipping her chin up as Luke relayed the message. "I'll get the men started then I need to talk to the foreman. Stay here with Luke and enjoy the colt. When you two are done come find me for lunch." Casually, Gabe slipped his hand beneath her hair, pulling her in for a hard kiss then left to go to work.

Jules rubbed her lips, surprised by how simply Gabe claimed them, as naturally as if he'd been doing it for years. This was just another sign he and Luke were not going to allow her to keep her distance.

"Did you enjoy your tour this morning?"

Jules turned her head to look at Luke. "You have a big spread, it's impressive. We didn't see much of it but I liked what I did see." She may have chosen a career in computers but ranching was in her blood. She knew a well-run operation when she saw one. Luke should be proud of what he had accomplished since taking over.

"Does it bother you having Gabe back?"

"What do you mean?"

Jules shrugged as the colt butted her hand, asking for attention. She petted his nose before explaining. "You've worked so hard to build up the ranch. I've heard my fathers talk about what a success it is. Gabe spent his time in the Navy, not working here with you. Now that he's back you two will have to share control. I was wondering if that bothered you."

"Gabe needed to get away. I understood that. Of the two of us he's the more intense one. I never planned on doing anything but coming back to run this place. After our parents retired and I took over, I kept Gabe up-to-date on the changes I was making, not the details but the general gist of what I had in mind. He always said he'd come home after he was done with the Navy. This is our ranch, not just mine. Gabe had a job to do serving our country and I had one here, taking care of the ranch."

"You don't resent him for that? For leaving you here? Wouldn't you have liked to leave the ranch, even for just a while, and see what else is out there?"

She was talking about herself, Luke thought, not him and his brother. Instead of calling her on it Luke kept their conversation light. She'd calmed down some since the night they'd brought her here and he didn't want to get her back up again. "This is where I live, what I wanted. Living on the ranch lets me free my other side as much as I like. But I can still leave, travel where I want to. No one is trapped here, Jules. Gabe needed to leave and roam the world, away from the Pride. I understood that. Just like he understood I needed to be here." Needing to touch her, Luke lifted his hand, tucking a lock of hair behind her ear. "Gabe being home is going to give me more freedom, not take it away."

"How so?"

"Knowing the ranch is in good hands I can travel if I want to. I can spend more time with the horses, less with the cattle. If I want to take a day off to shift and roam the ranch, I can. The need for control can strangle you if you let it, Jules. It can overtake you and color every decision you make. Having complete control over your life is an illusion. Learning to accept others in your life, giving up some of that control, it's actually empowering." Luke watched her closely for a reaction to what he said. The slight stiffening of her back, the straighter set of her shoulders told him she understood he was speaking not just about him, but her as well. "There's one more reason I'm thankful Gabe's back." Luke moved behind her, stretching his arms over hers as he linked their hands. "If he hadn't come back then I couldn't have you."

Luke surrounded her. Heat from his body spread to hers as he melted into her, his erection tucked tight against her ass, proving how much he wanted her. Soft lips worked their way down her neck then back up again along the curve of her jaw, each small kiss making her warm and ready for the next. Tingles of need began spreading through her body until the silent argument for keeping her distance stopped clouding her judgment and she turned her head, offering him her mouth.

Their kiss started slowly, a gentle mating game of lips and tongues. Jules closed her eyes as Luke played with her mouth. He tasted so good, better and sweeter than a ripe fruit. She knew she should fight harder to resist him. Clouding the many issues lying between the three of them with sex wasn't doing her any good; yeah, it made her feel good but did nothing to strengthen her resolve to make them see this mating was a bad idea. Like it was with Gabe or when the three of them joined together, the moment Luke touched her all thoughts of reason flew from her head. Maybe it was her moan, maybe it was his, the sound of need spread between them, telling them both a gentle loving was not enough. Giving up to what her body craved Jules turned in his arms asking him for more.

Luke gave her what she needed. Deepening the kiss, he wove his fingers through her hair, holding her still as he took her mouth. And she liked it, liked that he needed to taste her. Chest to breast, he pushed her into the stall door and settled his erection into the vee of her thighs. He felt so right, pressed against her tight like that. Kissing was good but she needed more. When Luke worked his hands between their bodies, brushing over her breasts and down her belly to unsnap her jeans, Jules deepened their kiss, just for a moment, then broke away.

"We can't do this here," she whispered against his lips. "Someone might see us." She wasn't refusing him, just worried about being out in the open where anyone walking by could see them.

"Come on," Luke growled, kissing her once more before pulling her down the aisle toward the rear of the stable. They stopped when Luke opened a door and pushed her inside a small room. When he turned on the lights she saw they were in some kind of supply room but he didn't give her time to look around. He backed her up against the door and took her mouth in a hungry, demanding kiss. Their hands flew between them, opening and discarding clothing, letting it fall to the floor.

Naked, Luke led Jules to a chair and small table she hadn't noticed before. Expecting him to put her on the table, he surprised her when he sat in the chair, spread his thighs wide and pushed her to her knees.

"Suck me."

Her eyes widened as she watched him take hold of his cock and stroke himself from base to swollen tip. *Damn, but he looks good like this.*

"I want your mouth on me."

She wanted it too. His cock was long and thick, the tip red and waiting for her mouth. Her tongue darted out as she lowered her head, swiping the swollen crest once, twice, before taking him between her parted lips. Jules closed her eyes as she went down on him. Bracing her hands on his muscled thighs she sucked him deep then pulled back. Encouraged by the greedy growl Luke let loose, she eagerly sucked him in again.

She felt his hand fist in her hair, guiding her movements as she pleasured him. Jules could tell he was holding himself in check, keeping his hips still instead of thrusting like his body demanded as her warm, wet mouth glided over his cock. The muscles of his thighs were tense under her hands. She wondered what she looked like, kneeling between his spread thighs, wondered what he thought of her on her knees, sucking his cock. The throaty sounds of pleasure he made told her he enjoyed her mouth on him and urged her on. He wanted her, wanted her to take him. When she reached between his legs and cupped his sac, he jumped and she purred, satisfied she affected him as much as he affected her. Jules protested when he pulled her head back and slid his shaft from her mouth before pulling her to her feet. He took her lips in a savage kiss as he backed her into the table. Lifting her, he set her ass on the edge of the table then pushed her to her back. "Spread your legs for me."

A flush stole over her skin at his request. He had seen her before, had fucked her before, hell she'd just gone down on him, but a sudden shyness overtook her, keeping her from doing as he asked. Just like it was with Gabe, the first time they'd been alone, Jules felt the difference from when they made love before, the three of them together.

"Jules," he coaxed, "it's just me." Luke ran his hands up her calves to cup her knees and gently ease them apart. "Open for me, baby."

"It's silly." She offered a small smile as she forced her thighs to relax under the steady pressure of his hands.

"It's not. You're not." Truthfully, he was touched by her reaction. This was her gift to give. When she finally relaxed and spread her legs wide enough for him to see the glistening folds of her naked sex, Luke knew this was a moment he would always remember. "You are so beautiful," he murmured, running the backs of his fingers over the smooth curve of her belly up to the generous swells of her breasts. "I want to learn everything about you, Jules. Tell me where to touch you."

"My breasts." He loved how she cried out as he took them

in his hands. Luke plucked at her nipples until they were red and hard, excited how they pearled under his touch.

His cock brushed against her sex as he leaned over her to lick the underside of her breast. "Where else should I touch you?"

"Everywhere," she sighed.

"I will, but tell me where I should start."

"Between my legs."

"Your pussy?" Luke lifted off her then touched the lips of her sex with the tips of his fingers.

"Yes. Don't tease me."

"Then tell me where you want me." He wanted her to say it.

"My pussy, Luke. Touch my pussy."

"Talk dirty to me, Jules." In that moment, which seemed like a lifetime, Luke thought she would refuse. He wanted to bury himself inside her until he couldn't tell where he ended and she began but before he could, before he took her, he needed her to do this for him. When she finally responded, her voice was low and soft, the sexiest sound he had ever heard.

"Part me so you can see all of me."

Luke's cock jerked as she spoke. He stroked the outer curve of her labia then used his thumbs to spread the lips of her sex. She looked so pretty he almost came right there and then.

"Am I wet?"

"Yes," he growled. So wet he wanted to taste her.

"No, Luke." She stopped him as he lowered his head. "I didn't say I wanted you to taste me. I want you to touch me."

"Show me where."

"Right here." She moaned, fingering her clit. "And here..."

Her fingers moved lower to the entrance of her body, stopped then pushed in deep.

He held her legs open and watched as she worked her body on her fingers like she did with his dick. "Fuck me..." This was the best thing he had ever seen.

"No, Luke," she countered. "Fuck me. Inside me, I want you inside me now, Luke." Jules pulled her fingers from her body, lowered her other hand between her legs and parted her sex for his use. "Fuck me now."

She didn't have to ask him again. Luke lined up his cock and entered her in one long stroke. He loved the way her pussy clamped down on him as he pushed past her resistance and slid home. He looked down and watched as he pulled out until only the swollen head of his sex remained inside her. Slowly he pushed back in until he was seated in deep and his balls rested against her ass. He moved like that a few times, teasing her, teasing them both then picked up the pace. Bracing his legs apart, Luke leaned over her body, held on to the table and shafted her, angling his hips up on each thrust, lifting her ass off the table.

Arching her body, Jules reached back over her head to grab the edge of the table, accepting his hard thrusts as he rode her. "More, more, more..." she chanted. "God, Luke...more."

He was almost there. Luke shut his eyes and threw his head back as she convulsed around him then let go, slamming into her and holding her still as he shot his load. Someone screamed but he didn't know who it was.

Jules batted his hands away as she dressed. "You're not helping, Luke." She laughed, pulling his hand out from the front of her jeans.

"I'm just tucking in your shirt."

"Tuck in your own shirt," she shot back. "Do you want everyone to know what we've been doing?"

Luke chuckled as he straightened his clothes. "Hell, Jules, one look at you and everyone *will* know what we were doing."

"What do you mean? Are my clothes on wrong?" She looked down to make sure everything was buttoned, tucked and right-side-out.

"I mean," he drawled, snagging her around the waist, pulling her up close, "you look like you just got fucked." Luke reached down to cup her ass, squeezing as he pressed close.

He was hard again, something Jules couldn't miss. "What are you, a rabbit?" She was going for stern but the words came out breathless. "You just got some." Jules tried to push him away but he held fast.

"A rabbit?" he choked out, thrusting his cock into the cradle of her thighs. "I'm all Lion, baby, and I'm hungry for more." Luke nibbled his way down her neck to the open throat of her shirt. "How about we find Gabe and move this to the bedroom?" He couldn't get close enough to this woman. Twenty minutes ago she'd drained him dry but here he was, hard as a spike and ready for more loving. Taking her by surprise, Luke lifted her up, nudging her legs around his hips until her ankles were locked together behind his back.

"Put me down, you fool." She slapped at his shoulder but couldn't hold back her laughter. "What are your hands going to think?"

Everyone who worked on the Roaring Lion was a Pride member. Her time here the past few days had not gone unnoticed. Rumors were circulating about why she was here. She'd mentioned it to Luke and Gabe, how it looked with her being here, but they told her not to worry.

Jules lowered her lids to half-mast as she looked down at Luke. The smile playing around his lips was a pale reflection of the one burning in his eyes. He looked so happy. A half hour ago he'd looked intense and feral as he pounded into her, giving her his cock while demanding her release. Now he reminded her of a man free of worries and wanting to play. This side of Luke she could handle. Oh, she'd take the naked one too, but this one made her want to smile back at him and see he got everything he wanted, just like she would for a kid with his nose pressed up against a toy store window the week before Christmas. She felt the same way about Gabe. She didn't understand it. It didn't make any sense. But right here, right now that's how she felt. Not wanting to ruin the mood, Jules pushed aside thoughts of the side of these men that scared her, the one that could take her independence.

"Let's go find Gabe." Jules pulled his head back as she lowered hers for a long kiss. "Let's see if he wants to play with us."

One kiss led to two which ended with her back against the supply room door being petted until she purred. She was disappointed when Luke got them out of there before things got out of hand and Jules found herself bent over the table with Luke taking her from behind, something he'd promised would happen the next time they fucked in the supply room. Still carrying her with her legs wrapped around his waist he strode through the stable then into the hot afternoon sun, whispering naughty sweet nothings in her ear. She was so caught up in the erotic imagery his words created she didn't realize he'd gone quiet and stopped moving until he tugged on her leg, urging her to her feet.

"Go up to the house, sweetheart," Luke told her, kissing her forehead absently as he looked over her head, watching as Gabe talked to two men across the courtyard. "We'll be up in a few minutes."

Puzzled by the shift in him, Jules looked up. Gone was the playful, sexy man who'd been taunting her with the promise of an afternoon in bed. In his place was a man on alert, ready to take on a challenge. Jules turned to see what had captured his attention then swore softly when she saw Gabe and who he was speaking with. Even from this distance she could tell they were arguing.

Mitch and Harlan Peyton. Jules took off, heading for the men, but was pulled up short when Luke grabbed her arm.

"Go to the house. Gabe and I'll take care of this."

"This involves me, Luke. They're here because of me. Don't expect me to wait inside like a house cat while you find out what they want." She jerked her arm, trying to break his hold but he wouldn't let her go. "I'd expect this kind of attitude from the Peytons. I never thought you'd sink to their level." It was a low blow and a nasty thing to say but it worked. Luke let her go. As they got closer she could hear what was being said.

"What makes you think you can come back after ten years and claim the Pride as your own? You've been gone a long time, man. You can't live with humans for all that time then expect to come back and be accepted as Leo. If you think—" Mitch stopped when Jules and Luke came around the truck. He ignored Luke. "Jules," he snapped. "It isn't appropriate for you to be here."

Jules was taken aback by the rabid look on his face. He'd gotten more demanding over the past few months, each time she saw him he'd become pushier and less willing to accept her blowing him off but she'd never seen him look this angry, not even when she hit him with her car. "What are you doing here?"

"We heard you were here. Heard Gabe was back. Harlan and I wanted to see for ourselves if it was true. You shouldn't be here with them, Jules. It doesn't look right."

"It's none of your business what I do, Mitch. I told you before I want nothing to do with you or your cousin." She looked past Mitch to Harlan. "I thought I made myself clear about that the last time I saw you."

"I don't know why you got pissed enough at Mitch to hit him with your car, Jules." Harlan dropped the cigarette he was holding and crushed it under his boot heel before moving closer. "I can smell the Becketts all over you. If you're willing to give them a ride why did you get all bitchy when Mitch and I asked you for one?"

"Don't talk to her like that," Luke snarled, pushing Jules behind him. "She told you she wasn't interested. Back off."

"Who the hell are you to tell us to back off?" Harlan shot back. "We've put up with her shit for three months. She knows we want her but won't put out. Now you two pick up her scent and she's willing to spread her legs and let you have a taste of what we've worked so hard for. If you get a taste so should we," he demanded, reaching for her.

Harlan's hands never touched her. One second he was reaching for her and the next he was on his back, his nose broken and spurting blood. Luke was pulling him back up with one hand fisted in his shirt and the other cocked back to deliver another blow when Gabe stopped him.

"I wouldn't," he warned Mitch as the other man made a move for Luke. Gabe never raised his voice, never moved a muscle but got his point across all the same, stopping Mitch in his tracks. "She *is* our mate. The mate call is over. The Leos are preparing the announcement now."

"You can't—" Mitch started.

"We did," Luke cut him off, letting go of Harlan. "The Leos accepted our mating."

"Fuck that." Harlan spat a mouthful of blood as he stood. "This is not your Pride. Mitch is right; Gabe can't come back after all this time and expect to take over as if he never left. The call went out and we answered it. The Leos know we want it. The Pride will be ours."

Jules had had enough. Before Luke could stop her she moved around him. "That's not going to happen, Harlan. It never was. I don't want you two. I told you that. Not only don't I want you in my life or in my bed, neither of you are fit to be Leos. You were never going to be my mates."

"We're not good enough for you but they are?" Mitch yelled. "What makes them so special? Gabe left the Pride—"

"Gabe served our country. He's done more with his life than either of you have ever done."

"They're no better than us, Jules. We have just as much money—"

"This isn't about money." The Peytons owned a successful dude ranch and tour guide business. "Leos need more than ego to run a Pride. They need integrity and honor and a vision for the future."

"You think we don't have that? You think they do?"

"I know they do. Luke and Gabe are two of the smartest, most honorable men I've ever met. They are strong enough to lead our people, Mitch."

"If they're so honorable why did they force you to come here?"

"They didn't—"

"Don't try to deny it. The story about how they brought you here is all over town."

"They may have brought me here but they haven't forced me to stay." And damn her, but somewhere during the past few days that had become the truth. "You and your cousin have tried to force me more than they have."

Jules knew she should have chosen her words more carefully when Gabe started growling like he was preparing to attack. The Peytons had to leave, *now*, before he beat the shit out of them. Just as she was about to order the cousins off the ranch, Gabe spoke up, not bothering to conceal his anger.

"It's time for you to leave. Get off our ranch." Something about the way he said that had both the Peytons stepping back but that wasn't good enough. Gabe took a step forward as Luke pulled Jules to his side. "Go. Now."

"This isn't over, Beckett," Mitch warned as he went to his truck. "We're not done with this."

When the truck was out of sight Jules spun on her heel and walked away from Luke and Gabe. The Peytons' visit killed the sexy mood she'd been in before coming out of the barn and reminded her that her will and wants were no longer her own to control. Having her pre-destined future and all the shit that came with it thrown in her face brought the anger and frustration back until it was all that she could see or feel. She started to cross the pavement, heading back to the house, but didn't get far before Luke stopped her.

"Jules—"

"Don't," she snapped. "I don't want to talk to you right now."

"You have to—"

"No, Gabe, I really don't. Oh, wait—" she turned to look at the brothers, snapping her fingers, "—that's right. I *have to* be mated. I *have to* get married. I *have to* be Lioness. Just like I *had to* change my plans and fall into line like a good kitty should. Well, you know what, guys? Right now I *have to* get away from both of you and the Peytons and my parents and anybody else who thinks they can tell me what to do." She jerked her arm away from Luke. "Back off," she snarled then turned and walked away.

Chapter Eight

It was a sign of respect that the Leos came to the Roaring Lion versus summoning Gabe and Luke to the Double K. Jules watched from the living room window as her fathers got out of their truck and walked toward Gabe and Luke, who were waiting for them by the main barn. The four men shook hands, acting like nothing was out of the ordinary. She wanted to be out there with them, to hear what they were saying. She should be involved in what was going on, she thought in disgust, not tucked away like a mindless housewife while her men saw to the details of her future. The only reason she remained in the house was because Gabe and Luke had asked her to. Asked, not told. It was a small difference, one a few days ago she may not have noticed, but it was an important difference, one she acknowledged in deferring to their request.

As the men disappeared inside the barn, Jules stepped back from the window. She knew why her fathers were here. Luke and Gabe had downplayed the Peytons' visit to the ranch, but she wasn't as naïve as they thought. After the scene in the courtyard both brothers put it aside, refusing to talk about it. Jules had been pissed by their attitude. Gabe might have been away for a long time but Luke had been around and was familiar with Mitch and Harlan. He knew what kind of assholes they were. If the penetrating looks Gabe had shot the cousins were anything to go by, he knew what kind of assholes they were too. The only time the Peytons' name had come up after they left the Roaring Lion was when Gabe asked her for details on her interactions with the other men. When she refused to give him any, he'd demanded she tell him. When Luke joined in, Jules felt like the top of her head was about to come off. Snarling over high-handed temperamental males, she'd walked away from them.

Walked away but didn't leave.

Instead of hightailing it off the ranch, Jules raided Jenna's closet for a bathing suit and spent the rest of the day by the pool. It wasn't until the sun's hot rays lulled her almost to sleep had she realized she could have left but chose to stay. Gabe and Luke had left her in peace, the first time she had been alone since they brought her to the Roaring Lion. With no one to watch her she could have run. Later that night as they ate dinner, then later still when they were in bed no one brought it up, not their unexpected visitors or her staying when she could have gone.

They also never questioned her about what she had said to Mitch about them. But it was there, hanging in the air between them, her comments about their honor and them not having to force her to stay on the ranch. If they asked about what she'd said Jules really didn't know what her answer would be. They *were* honorable men; she'd seen it and sensed it. Were-senses were a blessing at times, giving her the ability to sense deception. Luke and Gabe had never lied to her. She didn't think they ever would. Just like she couldn't lie to them about being forced to stay, not just because they might be able to pick up on it but because she'd be lying to herself and was done with deception after everything she'd gone through.

This morning she'd woken alone; another first since she came here. Even though it was early and there was no reason for her to be up, Jules had gotten out of bed and took a shower, still sleepy and only half awake. Their loving last night had worn her out. As angry with them as she had been, Jules did not refuse them when they asked her to go to bed. A few hours after she'd fallen into a satisfied, sated sleep, she woke as Luke penetrated her from behind, sliding his cock into her softened body while his brother slept on. It hadn't taken long for their strangled cries to wake Gabe, who then took his turn pumping into her pussy while Luke watched. Waking alone hadn't felt right, staying in bed by herself had felt wrong, so she'd pushed aside the need for more sleep, took her shower and went to find her lovers. What she didn't do was dwell too long on why she felt that way.

She found them in the kitchen drinking coffee and planning their day. When she walked in, Gabe leaned back in his chair to grab the coffee pot from the warming plate on the counter while Luke dished her up a plate of ham, eggs, and toast. It was easy, the three of them together sitting at the table eating breakfast and drinking coffee. No tension, no arguments, just a comfortable companionship as if they had been doing this for years. The issues hovering between them were pushed to the side for another time. Jules didn't think any of them were ready to deal with it right now.

The call came while they were clearing the table. Luke was laughing when he answered the phone, watching his brother playfully flick Jules with a dish towel while she ran around the kitchen trying to get away from him. Though the conversation she heard was one-sided it didn't take Jules long to figure out what was going on. The pleasant mood of the morning vanished. When Luke hung up and announced the Leos were coming over, the tension of yesterday was back.

Jules walked away from the window and headed for the kitchen to wait for her fathers to leave, the brothers to return, and for her to find out what her future was going to be.

"Jules," Gabe called out softly, letting her know they were back.

She was so absorbed in her thoughts she hadn't heard them come in. She looked up from the cup of coffee she'd let grow cold, watching as they each got a cup for themselves then joined her at the table. "What did they say?"

"Mitch and Harlan formally requested a mate fight. The Peytons do not accept our mating and demanded the right to challenge our claim. Nothing your fathers said changed their minds. They want you and are willing to fight to mate you. Mitch told the Leos they'd put too much effort in pursuing you to step aside."

"I already told them I wouldn't accept them as mates. They know I don't want them. I hardly know them, Gabe. Why are they doing this?"

Luke answered before his brother could. "They want the Pride. Don't misunderstand, they want you too, but more than that they want to be the next Leos."

She shook her head. "They are not leaders. They don't have what it takes to lead the Pride." She'd known that all along. Jules had never taken their bid seriously; not only had she never been attracted to them but she knew the Peytons didn't have the temperament to be Leos.

"Who would make the best Leos?" Luke wanted to know.

There it was, out in the open. If she answered honestly she was screwed. If she lied she'd be lying to them as well as herself. Calling on the stubbornness that got her in this mess to start with, Jules looked away and kept her mouth shut.

"When do you come into heat?"

Jules looked up at Gabe to find his jaw clenched tight as if he was checking his anger. She blushed at the question, which she knew was a ridiculous reaction considering the intimacies the three of them had shared. "Wednesday."

Like full-blood human women, Jules had the not-so-great joy of experiencing a period each month but as a WereLion she also went through a cycle of heat four times a year, during which she was able to become pregnant. Each cycle lasted a week. Barring any complications or medical problems, if she had unprotected sex during a heat cycle, she would become pregnant. Were-pregnancies were seven months long versus nine. Women of her species had the capability of bearing more children than humans but most chose to have two or three due to the usual strains having a larger family caused.

She didn't ask Gabe why he wanted to know her cycle. A mate fight and hunt required the participation of the female being fought over as well as the Lion or Lions involved in the challenge. All of them shifted into Lion form and since females could shift only during heat cycles or if they were seriously injured and needed to heal, that was when a fight/hunt was held. The sought-after female didn't fight. She was the reward. The winner of a challenge was declared when the other party either admitted defeat and submitted to the stronger male or when one of the fighters died. Regardless how the fight ended or who the winner was, the Lion or Lions turned on the female, running her to the ground to mount and claim their mate. To cement their victory the male would impregnate the female, binding her to him for the rest of their lives.

There was so much wrong with this, Jules didn't know where to begin. Frustrated, she got up, dumped her cold coffee in the sink, and stood staring out at nothing through the window. She heard them get up from the table and follow her, their heavy boots breaking the silence between them.

"Baby, talk to us." Luke brushed his hand over her hair.

"Don't shut us out."

For days she had been trying to explain to them how she felt and what was going on inside her head but they didn't want to listen. When it could have made a difference, they'd brushed aside her concerns and lulled her to them with sex. And she'd let them. She could have fought harder, could have tried to leave but she didn't. She took what they offered and had loved it. These two men made her feel things she had only dreamed about. Her feelings toward them had changed, that she would admit, but she didn't think she was ready for the rest of it; the commitment, the binding. Her biggest objection of being forced into something she wasn't ready for hadn't changed. If she had more time to get to know them and see how the three of them would settle into a life together, she could have handled it. Now it was too late. The mate call had started this, trapping her here, now the mate fight/hunt had her locked in. There was nothing she could do.

"Jules…"

She turned away from the window to look at them. Luke, Gabe, both of them looked sad, almost as sad as she felt. She thought they also looked worried, as if they weren't sure what to do next, or maybe what she would do.

"No one ever asked me what I wanted," she began quietly. "Not my fathers, not you. You may not believe this but I was never going to shirk my duty. Yes, I was going to leave the Pride for a while but I *was* going to come back. My fathers couldn't accept that. Years ago the four of you mapped out my future without asking me what I wanted or even consulting me." She paused, looking at Gabe then Luke. "Did you ever consider how I would feel about this?"

"You want us—" Gabe began.

"I did. I was, I *am*, attracted to you. Spending as much time in bed the last few days as we have you know that. But I want more than great sex from my future mates. I want to know there's more between us than physical attraction. You said I was stubborn and refused to go along with this...this, all this between us because I wanted my own way. That's not true. I knew I wasn't ready to be Lioness and all that came with it. Now it doesn't matter. What the Peytons did...it's over now. I can't put this off. You'll mate me, marry me, and make me pregnant." She ran her hand through her hair, pulling it off her face, trying to think of a way to make them understand what she was saying. "It's not just us anymore. If you win—"

"We will win, Jules. You don't have to worry about that." Luke's voice was more determined and harder than she had ever heard it before.

She didn't disagree; hearing him say it like that she believed him, not that she ever doubted the outcome of the coming fight. Gabe and Luke would kick the Peytons' asses. "After you win," she amended, "if you follow tradition, you'll get me pregnant. If you don't that could cause more problems. That means having a baby together when we hardly know each other. Have you thought about that?" Jules closed her eyes as tears pooled in the corners, part in frustration, part in sadness, and part at the image of holding a child she created with these two men; a beautiful baby with her smile and its fathers' eyes. She loved kids, always thought she'd have kids, but not now, not yet.

"Nothing would make me prouder than getting you pregnant, Jules. I've thought about it for three years. There is no other woman I would want to carry our children." He wanted it. The idea of her swelling with their child made him eager to take her to bed right now and practice the process. He wanted her to have their baby, watch her nurse it and love it. He wanted more than one with this woman. He wanted a family, a

Pride of their own.

"Would it be so terrible, having our baby?" Gabe asked quietly, wrapping his arms around her. "Maybe a baby girl who looks like you or a little boy who looks like us?"

"You don't understand..."

"We do, Jules."

Jules moved away from Gabe then brushed the tears from her cheeks. "I'm going to throw some water on my face then I need to call my mom. She'll want to know what's going on over here."

The guys knew she wanted to put some space between them but didn't call her on it. Before she left the room they each kissed her and were gratified when she kissed them back.

Luke pounded his fist on the counter while Gabe crossed his arms over his chest as they watched her walk out of the kitchen.

"She's right, you know. We fucked up, Gabe."

"Yeah, I know."

And they had. Both he and Gabe had been so focused on bringing her into their lives they never stopped to consider what kind of impact their actions would have on her. Neither had her fathers. Cherry had been right; they should have been honest with her from the beginning. All of them should have had enough faith in her to know she would never shirk her duty to the Pride. If they had established a relationship with her three years ago instead of going behind her back to her fathers to secure their claim, they could have eased her into accepting them and their future.

"What are we going to do?"

"There isn't much we can do. Are you willing to give her up?" Gabe asked him.

"You know better than that." There was no way in hell he would ever give Jules up. She belonged to them just like they belonged to her.

"Then we fight the Peytons, win and make this mating formal. Until then we back off."

It went against their nature to back off from any challenge but Jules didn't need any more pressure put on her right now. "She won't leave us." She may be fighting them but Luke knew she felt as strongly about him and Gabe as they did about her. She had to. He didn't think he could bear it if she didn't.

"I'm not worried about her leaving, Luke. I don't want her to pull away from us. The fight is in two days. Since she's been here we've kept her busy with sex or by talking about the ranch. She needs to learn more about us. That's what she wants so let's give it to her. We'll back off, keep things light and open up to her. You heard what she told the Peytons about us. She wasn't lying when she said it. The feelings are there. We've just never given them the chance to break through."

Luke agreed with his brother. They wouldn't let her go. No matter what happened she belonged to them. Now they had to show her they belonged to her just the same.

Chapter Nine

The next few days passed in a blur for Jules. She spent them at the Roaring Lion since there was no point in going back to her family's ranch. She stopped answering the phone Monday afternoon, sick and tired with the calls from friends asking her if it was true, wanting to know details of the upcoming fight/hunt, offering congratulations on her relationship with Gabe and Luke. Just as many Pride members came to the ranch, showing their support for Gabe and Luke, telling them they would be welcomed as the new Leos and the Peytons didn't stand a chance during the fight.

Her mother had come by, taken one look at her, pulled Jules into her arms and let her cry on her shoulder. Jules was grateful her mother didn't pass judgment nor did she press. No, her mom listened while Jules spoke and sat quietly while she paced. Jules had been surprised when her mother stopped short of asking her what her feelings for the Becketts were, but she knew why she did it; Jules had to ask and answer that question herself.

Both Luke and Gabe gave her space to work things out in her mind and accept what was happening but, even though they were off doing their own thing, she felt their presences as if they were by her side the entire time. Every thought she had, had them in it. When they were together, whether it was just two of them or all three, they talked, really talked for the first time since coming together. The brothers asked her about her life; her work, her friends, they seemed to want to know everything about her. And she wanted to know everything about them. They told her of their likes and dislikes, Gabe's time in the Navy, Luke's time on the ranch. They drew the line at discussing past girlfriends and outright refused to talk about any women they had shared. And in the dark, after they made love, they talked about their dreams and hopes for the future and Jules learned what they wanted out of life wasn't so different from what she wanted.

In the tradition of their people, the five of them were the only Lions in the pasture. The mate fight would commence the moment the moon reached its highest peak in the star-speckled sky. Jules glanced nervously between the two pairs: the Peytons a few hundred yards away, Gabe and Luke just off to her side. It had been years since a mate fight had been called in the Pride. Most members thought the practice was outdated, a throwback to the days when survival of the pack was more primal, when maintaining life literally depended on being able to stake a claim and fight for what you needed. She'd heard the stories of the brutality and the savageness and it scared her.

This was her fault. She couldn't deny it. If she hadn't been so stubborn about getting her own way and postponing her mating, her fathers would never have made the mate call. Gabe and Luke would have claimed her, mated her and no one would have had a right to challenge them. And their claiming, it would not have been a bad thing. After everything she had gone through these past months, all the time she'd spent thinking about her situation, there was one thing she never considered. She was a WereLion. Humans acted on emotion. Lions acted on instinct. Her inner Lion recognized her mates long before the woman in her saw them for the men they were. She'd been fighting a battle where the winner had already been declared by the shifter inside her. There wasn't much time but she had to make this right between them, the three of them, before it was too late.

Unease crept down her spine as she watched her lovers calmly take off their clothes, setting them aside as they readied to shift. She turned around and saw Mitch and Harlan doing the same on the other side of the pasture. Fear rolled off her in waves as the moon rose higher in the night sky.

"Jules."

She jerked at the sound of her name being called softly from behind. Turning back, she saw Gabe and Luke. She wanted to cry at the savage expression on both their handsome faces.

"Baby, don't look like that." Gabe pulled her close, drew her into his chest as his lips tenderly brushed her temple. "There's nothing to worry about."

"What if they—" she started. She *was* worried and it showed in her voice before Luke cut her off.

"This will be over quick. Don't worry about the Peytons." He ran his hand over the back of her head, cupping her gently. Stepping closer to her and Gabe, he lowered his lips to hers for a deep kiss. "Stay back by the truck, out of the way. Before you know it this will be over and we'll go home, together. Have faith in that," he ordered before kissing her again.

"But—" This time it was Gabe who cut her off with a kiss. Tears prickled behind her eyes as he loved her mouth, trying to take away her fear. She returned his kiss with everything she had in her soul. There was nothing more in the world she wanted than to make them both get in the truck and drive away from this madness. She wanted to be home with them in their bed, their bodies naked and ready for loving rather than fighting. They didn't have much time, which had her pulling her lips from Gabe's with regret. "I have to tell you both something," she started, looking from one of her mates to the other. "Before it's too late—"

Gabe captured her lips again for a short, hard kiss before lifting his head and looking down at her. "Don't think like that, sweetheart. Don't you have faith in us?"

It was said in a teasing manner but the expression in his eyes told her he was serious. He needed to know she had faith in him, in his brother. "I do. I have faith in both of you. But you need to know, I have to tell you—I lied before. That first night at the ranch, I lied when I said I didn't feel it too. Three years ago you decided to mate me because you felt the pull, the call. You knew it was right." Reaching out her hands, she cupped both their faces, her gaze darting between the two of them.

"So did I. Not that I wanted you for my mates, I didn't know that then, but I felt it too, what was between us. I dreamt of the two of you," she admitted. "When I thought of my future mates it was your faces I saw. And it scared me. That's why I wanted to run. I was so afraid I'd be...swallowed, consumed by the two of you...I got scared." She offered them a small, wry smile. "You have no idea how intimidating you are. Both of you. There is no one in the Pride better suited to be the next Leos than you two. I knew that. I was just too stubborn and focused on myself to accept it."

Gabe's chest swelled at her admission. He didn't have to look at his brother to know Luke's did the same. He breathed deeply, drawing in her scent, noting the subtle difference. She accepted them. Would yield to them and it flowed from her like the fragrant air after a sweet summer rain. "I love you, Jules."

"We love you," Luke added. "You are our mate."

"Yes," she said softly, "I am." Leaning into Gabe first, then Luke, she kissed them both, giving them her love. "I love you both. My mates."

As a unit, her loves stepped back. "It's almost time." Gabe looked up at the moon. "You have to get ready to shift."

Both men watched as she stripped off her clothes, placing them over the side of the truck. They weren't the only ones watching. Gabe would have cursed over the Peytons seeing what belonged to him and Luke but held back for Jules' sake. Even from a distance he could smell the other men's lust and it pissed him off.

"Don't," Gabe ordered his brother as Luke moved to shield Jules' naked body from the men across the pasture. "Let them look. Let them see what will never belong to them." Eyes focused on the other pair, Gabe reached out to Jules. Turning her so she was facing their challengers, he pulled her back into his chest. His cock swelled, prodding the softness of her ass as he wrapped one arm around her middle. With cool deliberation he ran his hand down her throat to her breasts, firmly cupping one then the other possessively.

Jules knew what Gabe was doing. Aided by the radiant light of the full moon, Mitch and Harlan had a clear view of her lover's hands on her body. It wasn't in her nature to be shy about her body. She had no desire to hide her nudity. The moan passing through her lips as Gabe reached her sex, slid his fingers through her moist folds to rest at the entrance of her pussy, was given freely. She ground her ass into Gabe's erection as he penetrated her. "Luke," she sighed, calling for him.

"I'm here, baby." Stepping closer he put his hands where his brother's had just been, lifting and cupping her breasts as he lowered his head.

Sweet pain lanced through her nipple as Luke took the

tender tip between his teeth. Nipping then licking, Luke ate at her breast while Gabe thrust inside her. Two hungry cocks, one pressed into her stomach the other nestled on her ass, taunted her. The way they were standing, the way their bodies were turned, allowed the Peytons to see everything.

"Gabe is right, Jules." Pulling his lips from her breast, Luke raised his head for a kiss. "Let them look. Let them watch us mark you."

That was the only warning she had. As one, the brothers licked the curves where her neck met her shoulders, Gabe on the right and Luke on the left. Shivers shot up her spine as their extended canines raked her skin, scraping hard enough to raise welts. The pain was fleeting, teasing her with the promise of more. Gabe pressed higher inside her aching pussy as he thrust faster; she arched into his hand, wishing it was his sex claiming hers. Every plea she made was useless; Gabe was content to tease her, taking her to the edge but keeping her hanging instead of letting her fly off. As her lips parted to beg for more, her pleas became sharp cries as twin sets of canines clamped down on the curve of her neck, piercing the skin to sink deep and true. It hurt as they left their mark, branding her as theirs. Tears leaked from her closed lids as their teeth retracted, replaced by soft healing licks that lapped up the blood seeping from their marks. Jules cried again as Gabe pulled his fingers from between her legs, leaving her achy and empty.

Enraged roars from across the pasture broke the sensual spell surrounding the trio. She had been claimed, mated and marked. The combined acts bound her to the brothers for the rest of their natural lives. The first two had been done in the privacy of their home. The last a public act, one done out of love, but done *now* as a means to stake their claim and announce their superiority. By marking her in advance of the challenge, Gabe and Luke had thrown down the gauntlet, showing the Peytons they had no doubt they would be victorious in battle. The brothers pulled away, each taking one last taste of her lips before pushing her behind them.

"There's nothing to worry about, Jules." Gabe ran his hands down her back one last time before moving away from her. "This is going to be over quick. When it's done we'll come for you. Be ready for us."

Energy flowed around the trio, spiking the night air with an electric charge as muscles and bones belonging to men transformed into powerful bodies commanded by the hearts of their Lions. Jules usually experienced great joy when she shifted, a calming peace at being whole before giving in to the need to run and roam. Tonight there was no joy; it had been replaced by fear and anger and a fevering wish her mates walked away from this unscathed.

They gave no warning, no roars or howls to signal the start. Jules watched with the piercing eyes of her Lion as her mates took the offensive and charged their opponents. They were hunters, predators, intent on proving their dominance. Luke took Harlan while Gabe faced Mitch and as a unit they attacked. Teeth and claws damaged muscle and bone as they fought. From across the distance Jules could hear the cries of pain as her mates tore into the other Lions. Each blow the Peytons managed to inflict on her mates she felt as if it was her flesh being torn open and bloody. She wanted to howl and roar into the night at the injustice of Gabe and Luke having to fight for the right to love her but she kept her cries buried inside, not wanting to distract her loves.

At times the Lions fought standing on their hind legs, using their teeth to bite and scrape. Her eyes flew between the pairs as claws flashed with their knife-like nails tearing into each other. The Peytons wanted to kill but lacked the strength to take Luke and Gabe down so they fought dirty, striking at wounds already inflicted, hoping to distract her mates with pain rather than overpowering them with skill. After what seemed like an eternity but in reality had only been a few minutes, Gabe and Luke pushed forward on the Peytons, giving them all they had and took them to the ground, demanding their allegiance with deafening roars. First Harlan then Mitch accepted their defeat by exposing their throats to the Leos, offering their blood and laying aside their challenge. Together Gabe and Luke let loose a roar that echoed throughout the hills of the pasture to the canyons and valleys beyond, announcing their victory to all who may hear it.

It was over.

They had won.

Torn and bloody, the two victorious Leos circled her smaller Lion. On the left, Gabe let loose a thunderous roar that pierced the air, staking his claim on the night and all creatures within its range. Luke let his brother mark their territory before joining him. He began with a low rumble that expanded to reverberate across the grassy hills, spreading far and wide. Tails twitching, backs ruffed, the Leos clawed at the ground, marking it as they approached her.

Acting on instinct, she turned and ran, eating up the earth with her powerful legs. Sleek muscles bunched and stretched under her coat, propelling her forward, away from the males who demanded she accept their claim. She ran not out of fear but in an automatic response to her DNA. Each male outweighed her by over a hundred pounds, their strides more than twice hers in length. There was no escaping them. She was meant to be caught. And she was.

Gabe flanked her right side, Luke had her left. Breaking forward on a burst of speed, Gabe shot around her to take the lead then turned to charge her, intent on halting her progress. Luke, his darker mane splayed and bloody from the fight, came up along her left side, butting her with his massive head, closing in on her body with his as he herded her toward Gabe.

They had her corralled and at their mercy. They surrounded her, deep rumblings reverberated from their chests. When they rubbed up against her they purred. Jules stood still and accepted their presence. Heat poured from their bodies into hers as they touched her. She wanted to lick their wounds and heal them but they didn't give her the chance. Luke and Gabe shifted back to human form and Jules shifted with them then let them have their way.

There was no foreplay and no one spoke as Luke took her to the ground, positioned her on her knees, pulled her ass up and entered her from behind. Heavy breathing and loud grunts filled the air around them as Luke staked his claim and exercised his right to mate her. Jules hung her head and braced her body on her arms as he rutted inside her. Her breasts swayed under the force of his thrusts but she didn't care. This was meant to be.

Just when she thought she couldn't last another minute Gabe stepped in front of her, pulled her head up and pressed the bulbous tip of his cock to her lips. Jules opened her mouth and sucked him in. He pressed forward until he hit the back of her throat. He used her mouth like Luke used her cunt. Relentless and forceful, her mates fucked her, showing her no mercy.

Jules loved every minute of it. Her climax when it came was stronger than she had ever experienced before. Her pussy contracted around Luke's thick cock, triggering his release. She would have screamed but Gabe's shaft plundering her mouth prevented any sound from escaping. No sooner did Luke finishing jetting his semen inside her did he pull out and switch positions with his brother. The tender inner tissue of her pussy ached as Gabe drove into her and used her sex like he'd used her mouth. Jules licked Luke's still hard cock and tasted their combined release. He fisted his hand in her hair, pulled down her chin and sank inside, demanding she take him. These men were primal and fierce as they fucked her and marked her body and soul. She came again as Gabe reached his own climax and flooded her with his seed. A moment later Luke came in her mouth and as she swallowed she drank in their roars, thankful they had chosen her.

They had claimed her.

She was their mate.

About the Author

Claiming Their Mate continues at www.paigemckellan.com. Stop by Paige's website to see what happens to Jules and her mates as they begin their happily ever after. Do they drive her crazy? Yes. Does she get even? Oh, yes. Are they happy? Absolutely. While you are there check out her blog, free short stories, introductions to new characters and much, much more. Paige loves to hear from readers. Send an email to paige@paigemckellan.com or paigemckellan@aol.com.

Rachel's Totem

Marie Harte

Dedication

To Angie, a great editor who's not as evil as her blog would tell you.

Chapter One

Cougar Falls, Montana

C-o-n-d-o-m. Worn in conjunction with sex. Take it into town, find a woman and use it, for God's sake, or we're not coming home.

Sincerely, Dean and Grady.

"Assholes." Burke Chastell discreetly pocketed the small foil package in his pants and crumpled the note in his fist, dropping it on the table in front of him. Idiot brothers. Grady must have written the note Burke had found folded and tucked into his shirt pocket. Dean could barely spell his own name, and "conjunction" was a three-syllable word.

So what if Burke had been a little testy lately? Since Charlotte Penny's death, the entire town had been waiting on pins and needles for a reading of her will. But damned if her attorney would tell them anything. Gerald insisted they wait for Rachel Penny, Charlotte's niece. A woman they'd never met, and who very likely wouldn't be able to find Cougar Falls, in any case.

Glancing around at the small semi-crowded diner, Burke nodded at several of his neighbors, hoping Mac might choose today to leave the kitchen and wait on some tables. Trying to focus on the menu he didn't need, Burke groaned inwardly when he scented the cloyingly sweet smell of the woman who'd been harassing him for years.

"Burke, how nice to see you this morning." Sarah Duncan interrupted his thoughts, and he quickly covered the ball of paper he'd crumpled on the table with a large hand. God forbid Sarah get her hands on that nugget of gold. The woman was constantly in heat, and he had no urge to dip his wick where half the men in the county already had.

Sarah filled his cup with steaming coffee and waited for an acknowledgement, one hand resting on a curvy hip.

He grunted, and she shook her head. "Cat got your tongue?" She smirked, batting her eyes as if the cleverest girl in the world.

Why had he chosen the Fox's Henhouse for breakfast today? He should have followed his instincts and driven the twenty miles into Whitefish instead of lingering in town.

"Funny, Sarah." He sounded as if he'd just swallowed a bucket of gravel, but he had no inclination to play this morning. He needed to get a handle on Charlotte's absent niece, on the Gray Wolves running amuck in Glacier, and to find that damned totem again before all hell broke loose.

Burke could feel the mystical totem's loss as keenly as the others. In the air was a void where the totem's strong spirit should have been protecting Cougar Falls. It was only a matter of time before the human populace took notice of the small town that "didn't exist". *Fuck.* He had to find that totem.

"Come on, puma man. When you gonna give me a little lovin'?" Sarah did her best to engage him, bending down to show generous cleavage as she stroked his forearm...*without asking.*

His hackles rose at the clear breach of etiquette. He might be a man, but he was a catamount as well, a feline Shifter protective of his space. Burke heard the chime of the door opening, but had his attention fixed on Sarah, in no mood for her games. "You couldn't handle me even if you wanted to. Back off, and get me the damned special. *Now.*" His growl alarmed the rest of the patrons in the diner, and he felt their stillness even as the rich aroma of fear wafted under his nose.

"Oh please. I guess even this far north the he-men are out in force."

The belligerent voice had everyone in the room turning to stare at the newcomer in shock. *A stranger.* In the Fox's Henhouse. In Cougar Falls.

"What? Is this a private restaurant, or can anyone order the 'damned special'?" The stranger, a woman, glared down her nose at Burke, then turned a warm smile on Sarah. "Is it okay if I sit anywhere?"

Sarah gaped dumbly until Burke nudged her. "Oh, um, yeah, sure. Have a seat wherever." She beamed and fled behind the counter, her whispered exclamations audible to everyone but the stranger who sat as far away from Burke as possible, in a booth with a view of the mountains as well as the rest of the diner. He sniffed the air, trying to catch her scent, and found to his surprise...nothing.

Just like Charlotte Penny.

His blood heated at the thought that he might finally have found a lead on the missing totem, and he studied the woman, absorbing what he could. She looked nothing like Charlotte, but that didn't rule her out as a relation. Charlotte had been a petite blonde, pretty in a soft, gentle way, and as wily as his grandfather.

This woman looked like an Amazon in comparison. Tall,

stacked and ferocious as she glared his way before studying the menu. Her hair was a long blue-black, shiny and straight but curled at the ends over her shoulders. Thick black lashes framed light green eyes looking out from creamy, golden skin. Her nose was thin and turned up at the end, saved from being just short of cute by the sexy-as-hell mouth curled in contempt at the moment.

He couldn't help lingering on her full breasts, their shape visible beneath the thin red T-shirt she wore. She obviously wasn't from the area, judging by her clothing, inappropriate for Montana's summer months. Even in July the sun refused to warm up beyond seventy degrees. Today's sixty-five was no exception.

Burke glanced around him to note everyone giving him the look that said, *Take care of her.* And once again he questioned the notion of having a catamount in charge of the totem's protection. The silver foxes were much better equipped to handle civilian authority and change. Both charming and sly, they'd been known to speak out of both sides of their mouths. Too bad his buddy Sheriff Ty Roderick presently had his hands full of the snotty wolf clan. Now if Burke could just keep Dean and Grady out of that mess waiting to blow up in their faces...

Sarah reappeared, breaking his concentration, and slammed a plate filled with food in front of him. She quickened her step to the stranger and began chit-chatting, fishing for information.

"Sorry it took me so long. That one there..." Sarah paused, nodding toward Burke, "...can be a bear before his eggs."

In the table next to him, Joel Buchanan snorted under his breath. "Bear, my ass. Cat has no sense of decorum."

Burke shot him a dark look that Joel ignored before turning back to his wife.

"I know all about his type," the stranger said, her lips fixing his attention.

Damn, but her annoyance was starting to turn him on. Granted, she was hot. But normally, animosity didn't have him half-hard. The woman didn't seem as affected. He could sense she felt anything but arousal. Anger burned through her pores.

"Ah, sure. He's okay, really." Sarah glanced back at him anxiously and he rolled his eyes. She turned back to the woman. "How about I bring you the special, and you can see why our customers are just so irritated to have it?"

The woman grinned and handed Sarah her menu. "Sure thing."

"So what brings you to our little town? Cougar Falls is kind of off the map."

An understatement. Cougar Falls was not only not on the map, but thanks to the totem on Charlotte's—what used to be Chastell—property, only Shifters and humans with the ability to *turn* could find the place unless brought along by one of the townsfolk.

"My aunt used to live here." A collective sigh whispered throughout the room. "Charlotte Penny? Maybe you knew her."

Sarah clucked and patted the woman on the hand. To Burke's perverse satisfaction, the woman tensed and slid her hand under the table once Sarah let her go, as averse to pawing as he'd been. He grinned and tucked into his food, his ears perked.

"Sure. Everyone knows—I mean, knew Charlotte. In a town this small, no one's a stranger." Sarah wiped her hands on her apron. "I'm Sarah Duncan."

"Rachel Penny." They shook hands.

Rachel. Burke stared at her. It fit. A strong name for a

strong woman. Now how to change the bad impression he'd unintentionally given and get the woman to sell him Charlotte's property?

Rachel did her best to ignore the hot stare running over her from head to mid-belly—what was visible before the table cut her off. Why hadn't she ignored the mountain view and sat with her back to the jerk? She couldn't help glancing up, only to see his eyes locked on her with an intensity that had her fuming...and glaring back out at the mountains as she tried to ignore the answering race of her pulse.

Why did every good-looking son of a bitch have to be such a creep? Her ex-husband had been an Adonis, and he'd not only cheated on her, but systematically wiped through their savings with his legal bullshit and games. Thanks to him, she'd finally settled her divorce with a whopping one thousand dollars to her name—and three months later less five hundred more—no house, no car, and what clients she'd managed to tear from their previous joint Internet business.

Sitting several booths down from her, the guy oozing sex appeal and a bad temper seemed worse than Jesse. For one thing, he was better looking with a better body. And that voice... Much as she felt annoyed, that irritation struggled against desire rising sharply out of nowhere. Tamping it down was harder than it should have been, but Rachel managed.

Mr. Bad Ass had sandy blond hair long enough to need a cut, giving him a bad-boy appeal. His eyes were a bright, whiskey brown, and his chiseled jaw and firm chin hinted at more than stubbornness—an attribute that never failed to attract Rachel. *I'm such an idiot. I shouldn't look at this guy. He's not what I need right now. I mean, come on. His attitude needs an overhaul...as does his seeming inability to look anywhere but at my breasts.*

"Anytime you're through undressing me with your eyes," she snapped.

Several grumbles sounded around her, one louder than the others, and she glanced around the diner to see a bear of a man choking on his laughter.

Bad Ass simply grinned, and her hormones shot into overdrive, making her warring lust and rage into a tangible thing.

His grin faded and he cocked his head, studying her with a deep scrutiny that had her feeling like prey. Muttering a curse under his breath, he pushed away his half-eaten plate, threw a few bills on the table and stormed out of the diner.

The minute he left, her libido subsided, and Rachel waited for her breakfast in relative peace. The rest of the locals left her alone, though she could feel the weight of their curiosity in the stares that refused to leave her. Natural enough in a small town, she supposed.

Sarah brought her the special, a cup of coffee and her ticket, and apologized profusely for taking so long. Thankfully, the touchy woman left without another word, allowing Rachel to finally satisfy her hunger...and dwell on the circumstances surrounding her newfound fate.

A year ago she'd thought she'd finalized the divorce with Jesse, only to have him drag her through court as he tried to swindle what he could out of their holdings. They'd never been rich, but they'd been comfortable, and happy, or at least, she'd thought so. Finding him screwing their accountant had proven her seriously wrong. And Linda wasn't younger or prettier than Rachel, which made it worse. Apparently, the backstabber was better in bed, because her breathy cries had alerted Rachel that something was definitely "wrong" with their accounts.

The quickie divorce she'd expected turned brutal as Jesse became the ex from hell. As if cheating on her weren't bad enough, he tried stealing from her as well. Six months of negotiating and he'd still managed to rip the company name away and nearly ruin her in the process. For God's sake, she'd brought *him* into their Internet web design company. Her baby from the get-go. Yet his fancy lawyer handed him the company's name, more than half their assets he hadn't already buried under false accounts, and her hard-earned reputation.

Rachel fervently hoped Linda gave him a disease, or better yet, an audit from the IRS.

Smiling into her eggs, which really were delicious, Rachel couldn't help remembering her Aunt Charlotte's raves over the diner's full, sit-down breakfasts, which brought back the sad predicament landing Rachel in Cougar Falls again. The last time she'd visited she'd been all of six years old, and she could still remember crazy old Aunt Charlotte whispering of the magic underlying the town.

As Rachel looked around her, she saw nothing supernatural or mystical. Only a small town with a surprisingly handsome populace, but nothing more out of place than a packet of sugar mixed in with the Sweet'N Low.

Aunt Charlotte had been a hoot, in all of the dozen times Rachel had seen her throughout the years. Charlotte loved her life and had never seemed to care what others thought of her odd notions of what might exist beyond that which people might see. The only times her aunt had left Cougar Falls were to visit Rachel, her favorite and *only* niece. First college, then her business had kept Rachel away. But despite their distance, the two managed to keep in touch via emails and phone calls, and Rachel had always felt a special affinity for the warm-hearted, open-minded woman.

Too bad I've finally come to see you, and you're no longer here.

Rachel finished off her breakfast and slowly sipped her coffee. According to Gerald Winter, her aunt's attorney, Charlotte had died peacefully in her sleep. She'd left her house and some property to Rachel, and a few other odds and ends that Gerald would read today in the will. Rachel, unfortunately or fortunately, depending upon her mood, had to be present to hear the legalities. She winced, recalling her last debacle with lawyers, the wounds still fresh.

Yet, it wasn't as if she had any other place to go. Her parents were dead. She had no siblings and few friends outside the ones Jesse had managed to steal after the divorce. Hell. The greater the distance between herself and her pitiful old life, the better. She'd spent the past nine months fighting, and the past three months licking her wounds. Wasn't it time to start over again? And with a clean slate this time.

Brooding over the optimistic idiot inside of her brewing with good tidings, Rachel gulped the last of her overly sweet coffee and glared at the packets in the center of the booth. Who ever heard of pink packets of *sugar*?

Grabbing her wallet out of her purse, she paid for her meal and left a tip for Sarah, then left the diner and its curious patrons behind. As she walked down the street toward her rental car, however, an altercation nearby forced her to stop.

Twenty feet down the alley to her right, Rachel saw the rude guy from the diner ducking punches from three overgrown bullies. Why she thought of the fight in those precise terms she didn't know, but she had a definite sense that Bad Ass was the innocent party. The fact that the huge thugs crowding him looked like walking wolf-men made it easier to portray the rude guy as the good guy.

Good lord, but how hairy and huge did they grow them up here? Bad Ass was at least six-four, and the men trying to pin him to the wall between them were as big if not bigger. All three looked like linebackers for a pro team, and they sported long, thick hair, beards and mustaches like mountain men from hell. One of them turned to study her, and even in the daylight his eyes seemed to gleam with a preternatural shine.

Shit. That is too weird. And this is way beyond my ability to make right.

Before she could call for help, Bad Ass slugged two of the men with fists so fast they looked a blur, putting his assailants down for the count. The remaining thug lunged at him, only to find himself suddenly plastered against the brick wall. Somehow, Bad Ass had used the thug's momentum against him, to his advantage. Throughout the fight, Rachel stood still, frozen by the animal-like grunts, brutal hits and sheer wildness frothing between the men. But when Bad Ass and then the other one started growling and...*hissing*...at each other, she took several steps back, thoroughly freaked out.

Had she not known better, she'd swear that thug was looking more and more wolf-like. And the cries coming from Bad Ass sounded feline, like a big cat howling a warning as his eyes narrowed, the color of his pupils reflecting an odd shine in the shadows of the alley.

A warm hand on her shoulder scared a mortifying squeak out of her, and Rachel spun around in a heartbeat. Seeing a badge, she breathed a sigh of relief.

"Easy, miss. I'll take care of this." The lawman tipped his hat at her and quietly spoke into his walkie-talkie, radioing for help. He walked toward the brawlers with an easy gait. Like the men in the alley, the sheriff had a feral quality about him. Something in the slant of his brows, the sharpness of his gaze and the readiness in his face. He sported denims and a work shirt, his hat worn from wear, but no gun belt that she could see.

Shorter than the men fighting by a few inches but no less muscular, the sheriff stopped a few feet in front of them. He said nothing, merely tapped his foot. When they continued to ignore him, spitting and knocking into one another, he crossed his arms and murmured something under his breath, and the two opponents sprang apart as if dashed with cold water.

"Burke, take Ms. Penny to see Gerald. He's waiting on you two. And Hart, you come with me."

The hairy brute grumbled but followed the sheriff without question, glaring over his shoulder at Bad Ass—at Burke. Four more men appeared at the mouth of the alley and dragged the two unconscious thugs from the scene. Deputies, maybe, though the four looked more like locals than lawmen. They spent an inordinate amount of time studying her, to her discomfort. And the strange, almost hungry looks on their faces had her taking a step back, only to bump into Burke.

Burke ignored her, however, and glared at the men moving the bodies. They hurried out of the alley, leaving Rachel and Burke alone. Together.

Not sure how she felt about being summarily dismissed by the sheriff, Rachel stared at Burke, her expression guarded as she wondered why she'd been left with such a dangerous man.

Burke scowled at her as he straightened his appearance. For a fight in which he'd been outnumbered three to one, he looked surprisingly none the worse for wear. Running his hands through his hair, he tugged the loose strands out of his eyes and tucked the denim shirt he wore back into his jeans.

Unable to stop herself, Rachel watched his long fingers inching under the waistband of his pants and couldn't help wondering if his skin felt warm even through a layer of clothes. A burst of longing, of animal need, rippled through her body and left as suddenly as it had come. She shivered, confused, praying Burke assumed it was from the cooling temperature.

Seeing her distress, he shook his head and grumbled under his breath. But to her astonishment, he shrugged out of his shirt, leaving him clad in a thin white tee and denims.

"Before you shatter all your pretty white teeth from chattering, put this on." He didn't give her a chance to refuse and enfolded her in the large garment. Oh crap, it smelled like him. And her libido, which had gone dormant in the diner except for one brief flare just moments ago, rose again with a vicious slap.

Having helped her into his shirt, Burke began to take his arms from around her when he suddenly froze, then stepped even closer. This near to him, Rachel couldn't miss the rising bulge pressing against her belly, or fail to note the quickening in his breath as she stared at his broad chest.

"Shit. I just knew you were going to be trouble," he rumbled before swooping down on her.

"What—"

He interrupted her with a soul-shattering kiss. Not gentle or tepid, Burke kissed like a man used to taking what he wanted. He devoured her, plain and simple. An explosion of scents and tastes, Burke was like a drug that stole through her body with the intent to possess. What started as hot grew to inferno proportions. His hard lips commanded, his tongue invaded and his body pressed her closer, until she was nearly riding the erection straining between them.

Without realizing she'd moved, she felt her back against a brick wall, Burke shoving his tongue down her throat at her garbled insistence. Lust took control of everything as the protestations and denials she should have spouted vanished under his onslaught.

A large hand palmed her breast, kneading the taut flesh before pinching her nipple. She arched into his mouth and cried out, her moans muffled by his kiss. Groaning, Burke lifted her in his hands, his strength a thing of beauty. Positioning her legs around his waist, he settled himself at the junction between her thighs and began thrusting against her, fully clothed.

Rachel shouldn't have felt much with panties and two pairs of jeans between them. But her strangely over-sensitized body didn't know the difference. The ridge of Burke's cock through his pants might as well have been touching her clit, since the nub spasmed with his every pressing graze.

Grunts and need poured from him as he catered to her every unspoken desire. He dominated, accepting nothing less than her complete submission as he pounded into her against the wall, his skilled fingers gripping her ass as he tried to get closer.

Common sense tried to reassert itself. Her ex-husband. Burke's like-minded arrogance. The fight she still didn't understand... All of it refused to surface as a ripping climax tore through her like a tsunami.

Obliterating everything, her orgasm took her into another state altogether. Colors and scents seemed sharper, sounds louder, and the feel of Burke against her like perfection made real. Rachel stiffened, twisting her ankles around his back, her thighs like a vise. Burke rasped and rained kisses down her neck, sucking hard at her throat as she panted, trying to catch her breath. His thrusts increased and he bit her neck hard enough to draw blood. The pleasure in the start of pain shot her into another orgasm, this one peculiarly forced, and oddly like an out-of-body experience.

"*Fuck.*" Burke snarled, shuddering against her as he came, jerking while his gasps of pleasure warmed her all over again. His scent drifted to her from his shirt, and hell, from Burke himself. Surprisingly sweet and definitely sexy, he made her think of caramel corn and hot, naked sex on a stick. A circus of delights brought to her by a man she'd only minutes ago wanted to slap in the face.

As she gradually returned to reality, Rachel blushed with embarrassment. What the hell had she been thinking to have sex with a stranger? A man who seemed very much like her ex-husband, at least at first glance. A familiar anger returned at thoughts of Jesse. But as much as Rachel wanted to blast Burke for taking advantage of her, the blissful look on his face held her tongue. That and the truth—that they'd both been helplessly ruled by lust. A first in Rachel's life, to be sure.

Burke finally released her hips and allowed her to slide down his body. His eyes flamed at the short contact between them, and Rachel gasped when her desire spiked again. *This is so not normal.*

"I, ah..." Burke trailed, seeming at a loss for words. But he didn't step back to give her any room. His gaze roamed her face, coming to rest on her mouth. The awkwardness she anticipated disappeared, and he grinned and nipped at her lips. "You are the sexiest thing I've ever laid eyes on."

Flushed at the compliment, she couldn't help wondering if she'd just made the next notch on his bedpost. Would he rush around to tell his buddies that he'd just dry humped Charlotte's niece in the middle of an alley? He was a man, after all. She'd been married to one who'd turned into Mr. Hyde. What did she really know about Burke?

For that matter, what did she really know about herself? Burke might be married. The fact that she hadn't even asked spoke volumes, and she suddenly paled, realizing she'd just acted no better than Lisa, her ex-accountant. Except at least Lisa had had the foresight to screw Jesse in her own office, behind a closed door, and not in an alley in a weird little town.

At Rachel's distress, Burke's smile faded. "It's okay, Rachel. We're two consenting adults. Both single." He stared at her ringless finger with his brow raised in question.

Something within her released. At least she hadn't climaxed with someone else's husband. Burke was staring at her, waiting, and she nodded.

"Definitely single."

"Good." He exhaled heavily, running his hand through his hair in agitation. "Look, you don't know me, *yet*, but I don't fu— ah, I don't normally fight and have sex in the alleyway before lunch."

The absurdity of his statement surprised her into a dry laugh. "What, you wait until the afternoon to have sex? Or you don't do it in an alley? Behind the restaurant more your style?"

That killer grin of his reappeared, a charming dimple winking at her from his left cheek. "We didn't exactly get off on the right foot this morning, and I'm sorry about that. But I'm not sorry about this."

The worry she'd been feeling faded at his warm smile, and she took a moment to revel in her relaxed body. She felt wonderfully sated after being deprived for a year and a half, and she couldn't help noticing the new and improved Burke... Burke who? Hell, she'd actually had sex with a guy without knowing his last name. Desperation at its finest.

She felt her cheeks flame. "Who exactly are you?"

Burke stared into her eyes for so long she thought he wouldn't answer. But when he did, he sounded distracted. "Burke Chastell. My brothers and I own the Catamount Ranch a few miles outside of town." He ran a finger over her cheek, making her traitorous body tremble. Leaning close, he shut his eyes and inhaled. "You smell like heaven. Hot and wet and addicting. And you have a body made for loving." He rubbed his cheek against hers before pulling back, his smooth face incredibly erotic against her skin.

She blinked, stunned at the man waxing poetic. When he opened his eyes, however, her throat went dry. The pupils staring out at her were slitted—*inhuman*—and he shocked her anew when his body began to rumble.

"Dear God, your eyes... Are you purring?"

Chapter Two

Burke shook his head, alarmed that he'd lessened his guards to such a degree. He'd almost fucking *turned* in front of Rachel, in front of a stranger who had no idea of what he was.

But her scent... In the diner she'd smelled like nothing, which in and of itself was enough to draw a second look. But now he didn't know what to think. He'd never taken a woman in public, and in a damned alley where anyone could have walked by and seen them. Burke wanted to blame his lack of control on the fight with the gray wolves, or even on his recent dry spell with the ladies. But the truth was, from the moment he'd seen Rachel Penny he'd wanted her. Her prickly exterior hid a well of untapped sensuality, and a spirit ready to know its inner beast.

And if she was anything like her aunt, then Rachel could assume any shape she wanted to if she found that damned totem before a Shifter could mark her. The thought of Rachel becoming wolf was unthinkable, especially now that he'd had a taste of her. She would make an incredible feline. But did he want to go so far as to mark her? To seal her fate as a cat Shifter and tie her to his family, if not as his mate, then as a member of his pride? And more, would she want him to?

But the real burning question...did Rachel know the truth about Cougar Falls and its special inhabitants? From the shock and fear in her eyes, he thought not. Had Charlotte confided anything about the town to her niece, Rachel wouldn't be staring at him as if he had three heads. Which brought him back to the matter at hand.

Blinking rapidly and forcing his breathing to even, he stopped his change. Focusing, he took a step back, mentally grimacing at the unwanted inches between them.

"What's wrong with my eyes?"

She stared at him. "They were...you looked..."

"Rachel? Are you all right?" he asked gently.

"I must be seriously losing it," she mumbled, shaking her head. "I could have sworn you—ah, never mind. It's been a long trip to Cougar Falls. And that fight earlier, and what followed after, shook me up." She glanced behind him, refusing to meet his gaze.

"I'm sorry you had to see that, Rachel." But he really wasn't. What could he say? *I'm glad you went into heat around me. I had to fuck you or go insane, and I can't wait to do it again, to feel that pussy squeezing my cock. I want you so much I'm hard again.* Or maybe, *Come on baby, say yes. Let's go fuck like rabbits until I mark you, and then we can live out our days together as cats on the prowl.* His eyes widened at the desirable, thoroughly unwise thought of mating with her, a woman he barely knew.

Even if she was the best fuck he'd ever had, Burke didn't do strangers. *And*, his conscience added, *you've never before experienced such urgent need.* So why now? And why Rachel?

Something about her called to him on a primitive level. He wanted to claim her, to possess that untamable quality within her. To soothe the hurt and anger that even now thundered in her expressive gaze, needing an outlet.

"Rachel, you might not believe it, but I don't normally do this." He waved a hand between them.

"You just did 'this'."

"So did you," he said quietly, trying not to sound accusing. "And though I don't know you well, I can sense you're not the type of woman who takes so quickly to a male."

"No, I'm not." Her cheeks turned a pretty rose-pink again. An Amazon who blushed. Burke's heart hammered, his instinct to hold onto Rachel and never let go almost frightening. "I can't explain this."

"Don't try. Let's just accept it for what it was." If only he knew how to define their meeting of minds and, well, almost-bodies.

"Ah, sure." She cleared her throat and hugged his shirt tighter around her body. "Oh, and thanks for the loan of your shirt."

The angry woman from the diner had all but vanished, leaving a charmingly vulnerable woman in her wake. Talk about fan-fucking-tastic sex with benefits. Burke wanted her again, right now, skin to skin. But seeing the defensive way she stood, the shields in her moss-green eyes resurrecting, he sighed and stepped back a few paces.

He grimaced at the feel of wetness sticking to his cock and underwear. Good lord, he hadn't come in his pants since high school with Missy Morgan behind the bleachers. Immediately he had a vision of Rachel and those bleachers, and as his cock stirred, he quickly readjusted his thoughts, blurting the first thing that came to mind. "Ty told me to take you to Gerald, Charlotte's lawyer."

"Right." Some of the pleasure leached from Rachel's face. "Aunt Charlotte."

Burke wanted to smack himself for being insensitive, but he was still tingling from coming so damned hard, and his new arousal was becoming painful. "I'm sorry for your loss, Rachel. I knew Charlotte as well as anyone around here, and I know she doted on you."

Rachel blinked. "She talked about me?"

"Only all the time." Burke took Rachel by the elbow and stiffly walked her toward Gerald's office. "Said you were the spitting image of her brother. Got all the looks in the family." He winked, and Rachel smiled prettily. "Also said you were stubborn as a mule."

"That's the truth." She sounded sad, and he cursed himself for making her feel worse when his intention had been to make her feel better.

They reached Gerald's building, and Burke knew he needed to prepare himself for whatever outlandish preparations Charlotte had made in her will. It was too good to be true that the woman would have simply willed him the property, the totem, and all that went with it.

Burke opened the door and followed Rachel into the converted post office. As steadfast as their odd little town, though in a new location, Winter and Sons had been servicing Cougar Falls since its official inception one hundred and fifty years ago. Gerald was the seventh Winter to head the law firm, and just as vigilant in serving justice as his father had been before he retired. Burke narrowed his gaze as Gerald walked out of his office and straight toward Rachel, a huge, predatory smile on his face.

A silver fox like the sheriff, Gerald did his best work soothing folks and maneuvering his way around the law. Women found him pleasing enough, and his profitable enterprise didn't hurt him for companionship. In his mid-thirties and a fellow schoolmate growing up, Gerald, along with Ty and Joel, made for interesting companions when Burke's brothers drove Burke crazy enough to leave the house.

And speaking of crazy... Burke glared at the sly lawyer cozying up to Rachel. Fortunately for Gerald, Burke was in a forgiving mood. Instead of ripping his throat out for poaching on Burke's territory—Gerald would clearly be able to scent Burke all over Rachel—Burke turned his roiling lust into fury, and kept it simmering just under the surface.

He growled under his breath, and Gerald swung wide eyes toward him, as if just noticing him. *Wily bastard.* Burke bared his sharpening canines and huffed audibly, shooting a small nod in Rachel's direction before turning fully human again. Hearing him, she turned and raised a brow in question. Gerald, however, took the hint and subtly stepped closer to Burke and away from Rachel. The lawyer extended a hand and shook hers, then just as quickly let go.

"I'm so sorry for your loss, Rachel."

His sincerity was clear, and Rachel tried to smile as her eyes welled with tears. Catching her by the elbow, Burke led her after Gerald, who motioned for them to follow him into his office. His paralegal was nowhere to be found, and Burke wondered where she'd gone to.

Seeing the question in Burke's eyes and his glance toward Julia's empty desk outside, Gerald shrugged. "Had a family emergency, she said. She'll be gone a week or more."

"Nothing serious, I hope." Burke liked Julia. A quiet fox, she kept to herself and always had a pleasant word for him. And even better, she'd shot his brother Grady down a dozen times or more.

"I'm not sure." Gerald frowned and shook his head. "I'm sorry, Rachel. Not exactly polite to discuss other matters when you're here for Charlotte's will."

"No, that's okay. I'm in no rush."

Well I am. Burke took a seat next to Rachel across from

133

Gerald, who sat in a huge leather chair behind his desk. *Let's find that totem and get back to the important things in life. Like how I'm going to seduce Rachel before she turns all prickly again.*

"It's just that my assistant, Julia, is always a rock, always here and helping. And something came up with her family in Washington so she had to leave yesterday—"

"Gerald, can we please get on with this?" Burke sighed.

Gerald cleared his throat and smiled apologetically. "Right, well. Before we begin, is there anything I can get you, Rachel? A glass of water, a soda, or maybe some coffee?"

Rachel shook her head. "Thanks, but Burke's right. Since we're here, no sense putting it off any longer. You might as well tell me what Aunt Charlotte wanted done with her things."

"Of course."

Nice how the SOB completely ignored Burke, who could have used something to drink. In a steady drone, Gerald read through most of the generalities of the will. All of Charlotte's personal possessions and money, investments and the like, went to Rachel.

"And as the only relative Charlotte truly cared about since your father passed away, you've inherited everything she considered dear to her. Including the house."

Shit.

"The property, however..." Gerald paused, and Burke wanted to punch him for drawing this out. "The property is divided between you and the Chastells." Gerald turned to Burke. "You've been wanting to buy from Charlotte forever. Well, Burke, now's your chance. If Rachel decides to sell, everything on the property, to include the house and the material within it, becomes yours." *The totem,* he meant but didn't say. With the totem back in the hands of protectors who both understood and respected the ancient relic, peace would surely return to Cougar Falls. No more clan wars, and no more threats of strangers having a hold on something as valuable as the totem.

Rachel stared at Gerald, her gaze narrowing with suspicion as it lit on Burke. "Are you saying Mr. Chastell wants my aunt's property? And that she steadily refused to sell it?"

Burke had a sudden ache in the pit of his belly, a feeling that often preceded something bad about to happen.

"That's what I'm saying." Gerald stacked his papers and squared them. "Charlotte's property and the Chastells' border one another. They've always been friendly, don't get me wrong. But it's no secret Burke and his brothers want to reclaim the land that their great-great grandfather gave to one of your relatives so many years ago."

"I see." She glared at Burke, and he stared back, confused.

"What?"

"Nothing," she snapped. Turning back to Gerald, she pasted a sugary-sweet smile on her face. "So the house is mine, and the property is split how?"

"It's a bit complicated. I'll drive you out to the property so I can show you both. Charlotte was very clear about this." Gerald turned sharp eyes on Burke, as if willing him to listen.

Burke, however, didn't understand what the hell had crawled up Rachel's ass. He couldn't deny her fury made him hot, but he didn't understand what he'd done wrong. Was she suddenly blaming him for their time together in the alley? It wasn't as if he'd staged that fight with those knuckle-dragging wolf Shifters. And he sure as hell hadn't planned to come in his jeans while dry-fucking her against a dirty brick wall.

"Burke, I said I'll drive Rachel out to the property now. Perhaps you'd care to follow, so I only have to do this once?"

Burke nodded. "Fine, sure. Look, why don't you go file your papers or something? I need a word with Rachel."

"Yes, Mr. Winter. I'd like a word with Mr. Chastell as well." Rachel's glare could have cut steel.

Gerald glanced from Rachel to Burke and unsuccessfully masked a grin. "Fine. I'll be waiting outside when you're through." Grabbing his papers and shoving them in his briefcase, he left the room, closing the door behind him.

The minute he left, Rachel stood ramrod straight and glared down her sexy little nose at Burke. "You arrogant asshole."

"What's your problem?" Burke honestly had no idea why she'd grown so upset.

"You thought screwing me would sway me into selling my aunt's place to you?"

Burke scowled. "Now wait a minute, Rachel. I—"

She leaned down and poked him in the chest, *hard,* stirring his instincts to fight back. Or perhaps, to turn their tussle into something more...intimate. "You wait a minute, Chastell. If you wanted to buy the place, all you had to do was ask. That scene in the alley was totally unnecessary. And not that good to boot."

He launched himself out of his chair to glare down at her. "Not that good, *Miss Penny?* First of all, that 'scene' in the alley, as you put it, was not staged. Second, that was anything but a real fuck. We had all our clothes on, for Christ's sake. And third." He paused to close what little distance remained between them. Staring directly into her eyes, nose to nose, he growled his last words. "The orgasm we shared was more than good, it was explosive. Lie to yourself if you want to, but you came hard, like a shot." He licked his lips, unable to help how turned on she made him in her anger. "And I can still smell your come creaming your panties. Hell, right now you want

136

nothing more than a hard fuck right on Gerald's desk, isn't that right?"

Her pupils dilated with lust, and her scent filled the room. Pure, unadulterated sex.

"Fuck. You."

"Sure thing, honey. You just name the time and place."

He watched in amazement as her pupils began to elongate. He could smell the familiar scent of feline musk flooding the room and waited, his breath held, as Rachel amazingly began to *turn*.

Her hair began to rise as her body was covered in a field of static energy, and her teeth grew sharp as she hissed at him in anger. God, she made him burn. The mixture of mountain lion and woman was almost more than he could take. Glancing at Gerald's desk, Burke figured he could have it cleared in one swipe of his arm. He'd bend her over the solid oak on her belly and yank those jeans and panties off her legs. Within seconds he'd lower his own clothes, just enough to spring his cock free before he'd shove it hard and deep into that honeyed, wet pussy.

Rachel's hands fisted into paws as she raised one arm as if to strike.

Do it. Please, touch me and I swear I'll mark you as one of mine in a heartbeat. The choice, even unknowingly made, had to be hers.

Gerald, damn his ass, chose that minute to knock at the door. "Hey, is everything all right in there?"

Son of a bitch. Burke knew Gerald could smell the passion raging in the room, the scent of a female in heat overpowering enough to easily reach the lawyer outside the office.

Rachel blinked, and that suddenly her shift vanished as if

it had never been. She swayed and righted herself, still miffed enough not to want Burke's touch. "Come near me again and I'll geld you." Sniffing, she turned on her heel and stalked out the door, nearly knocking over Gerald, who waited impatiently on the other side.

Gerald watched Rachel go with amusement, his lips quirked in an aggravating smirk.

"Not one word." Burke stormed through the door, knocking Gerald into the wall as he passed, heading for the bathroom to finally clean up. "Not one fucking word."

Rachel was so mad she wanted to cry. Frustrated anger that had no outlet, not to mention the absurd hurt, lingered in her battered heart. When would she learn? Jesse, apparently, hadn't been enough of a fiasco to teach her abject lessons about the male of the species. Men weren't loyal, they weren't honest, and they certainly weren't worth a single tear.

Wiping her cheeks with a rough jerk, she stalked outside to the only car in the lot and waited. Why couldn't she have seen this earlier? Men like Burke Chastell had one thing on their minds and one thing only: screwing over women to get whatever they wanted. Hadn't she caught him verbally abusing that poor waitress this morning? And the entire diner had overheard Rachel state her name as Rachel Penny, not to mention her connection to Charlotte. Why then hadn't he mentioned he wanted her land? That he and her aunt were neighbors, at least?

No. It was so much easier, and probably more fun, to fuck with Rachel's body and mind. The dishonesty of it all made her want to puke. It was so...so Jesse all over again. And then to stir her to horny madness in Gerald's office? What was wrong with him?

Shit. What was wrong with her?

Because as much as she'd hated him at that moment, her body had been readying for his penetration. Her clit ached at his nearness, moisture pooling between her thighs as if he'd had his large hand rubbing her, prepping her for his thick, juicy cock. She'd felt an almost animal hunger and a hazy sense of desire, both foreign feelings that scared her and aroused her all over again.

She groaned, clenching the hair by her temples. She swore she could smell him, even here. That caramel, sticky-sweet scent drenched in sex that made her want to spread her thighs and beg for him. *Beg? The only dumbass who should be begging is the jerk in that office. Creaming for him. Ha.*

Lie, lie, lie, her inner self urged her. *At least preserve your self-respect.*

Inhaling deeply, Rachel strove to work her temper under control. She refused to surrender to her body's foolish demands. Head over heart, mind over matter, and reason over orgasm should have been her steadfast mantra. Instead, she battled her desires as she waited for Burke the Jerk and Gerald to join her. But surprisingly, after just a few minutes, her raging need settled as if it had never been, making her more confused than ever.

When Gerald arrived a few moments later, he smiled and opened the passenger door of his Range Rover, waiting for her to enter. It felt strange to have a man behave like such a gentleman after Burke's aggressiveness and her ex-husband's perfidy.

Gerald, however, behaved with a gentle assertiveness she found comforting. He drove slowly through the town, commenting here and there on Cougar Falls' history. And she breathed easily, relaxed around him. Though attractive and with that same earthy scent all the men around this town seemed to possess, he didn't make her crazed with lust. She had no urges to strip him naked or nuzzle his neck to inhale his scent. Thank God.

"And there's Millie's ice cream parlor." Gerald pointed her toward an attractive little shop. "The woman's nearing seventy-four and still opens the shop every morning and closes it every evening. That's what I love about this place. The sense of pride in ownership and the family traditions."

Rachel nodded, taken with the charming town. The brick-and-log buildings showed their age and their character, all of them carefully preserved and well tended. She didn't see a speck of litter anywhere, just clusters of bright multicolored flowers in window boxes and barrels. As they neared the center of town, she saw groups of smiling and laughing couples with children dancing near what appeared to be an open park. In the park's center stood a large white gazebo peopled with musicians and surrounded by food booths.

"The Totem Festival's today. That's what has all those people out here so early on a Saturday."

"Totem Festival?"

Gerald smiled and kept his eyes on the paved road that gradually turned into a dirt road a mile outside of town. "A long time ago this used to be Salish land, though a lot of the history books show the Salish Indians farther west, thanks to our unscrupulous Uncle Sam." He grimaced and continued. "Well, a few Salish ran into a mysterious, small group of people inhabiting the region we now live in."

Rachel listened, curious and caught by Gerald's rhythmic words. She had a feeling the story was important, but couldn't have said why. When he'd mentioned the Totem Festival, her entire body tensed on alert. Like everything else that had happened to her since stepping foot in Cougar Falls, this made no sense either.

Instead of dwelling on it, she said to hell with worry and latched onto his story. "So the root of this festival isn't the Salish, but the people they ran into."

"Right, the Shifters." Gerald flashed her a smile and turned down another dirt road, taking them deeper into the mountains. "The Salish called them Ac-taw, which in the Shifters' language meant animal souls. According to legend, the Ac-taw could transform into the beasts that dwelt within their souls."

"What, like werewolves and cat people?" Funny, she'd heard the same tales from Aunt Charlotte growing up. But her aunt had never given the Shifters a name. She'd just laughed and teased Rachel with fanciful stories.

"I guess you could call them that. But the Indians believed more in a transmutation of souls into living form. Not so much monsters as people who could live as either animal or human, a beautiful combination of both spirits in one flesh." Gerald's words took on a dreamy tone, and Rachel had to force herself to recall he was telling a story and not some personal history.

"So where does this totem come in?"

"The Ac-taw supposedly worshipped a living stalk of wood that brought good health, long life and protection to those under its spell. And that living stalk of wood is the totem we celebrate on festival days."

"Days?"

"Four times a year the town celebrates the Totem Festival. It's fun, a way of ushering in the seasons. We have a carnival of sorts, nothing weird. The kids have a blast, and it's an excuse for the town's citizens to get together and have a big party.

"The totem's a beautiful antique, a large timber maybe twenty feet high and three feet wide. Animal carvings painted in rich, vibrant color decorate the thing. You can almost believe the legends about the Ac-taw having imbued the wood with their power. It feels incredibly alive. Once you've seen it, you'll understand what I mean."

"Wow. I'd like to see this thing. A magical totem pole and Shifters, huh? Cougar Falls has an entertaining history, I'll give you that."

Gerald grinned. "As do our inhabitants. You've met a few this morning, I gather."

Apparently, news traveled fast in a town this size. She wasn't surprised. "Yeah. I walked into the Fox's Henhouse ready for a big plate of pancakes only to hear Burke Chastell growling at some woman to keep her hands off. God's gift to women," she muttered, realizing how much she'd liked Burke's hands on her and wishing she didn't.

"Well, don't judge Burke too harshly concerning Sarah." Gerald continued to maneuver through a cropping of woods, confusing Rachel with the many twists and turns onto expansive dirt roads that looked no better than well-worn trails. "Sarah Duncan is not what you'd call a one-man woman."

"So it's okay to treat her like crap because she likes men?" Gerald wasn't looking so charming now.

"No, no." He frowned at her before turning his attention back to the road. "Sarah's a wonderful woman, though she's not really selective about who she sleeps with. But that's her business and no one else's. My point is, she's been all over Burke for years. No matter how many times, and nicely I might add, he's said no, she just won't leave him alone. And I don't know if you noticed, but he doesn't like to be touched."

That she hadn't noticed—at all. But maybe his reaction to Sarah had been justified, if what Gerald said was the truth. Which still didn't excuse Burke from screwing around with her to get at Charlotte's property.

"What about Burke? What's his deal?" She clenched her jaw at Gerald's knowing look. "I just want to know about my aunt's neighbor, that's all. She never mentioned him and I find that curious."

"Did she tell you a lot about us, about the town I mean?"

"Not really." The more Rachel thought about that, the more her aunt's omission struck her. "She used to tell me stories about what you called Ac-taw, or Shifters. Interesting fantasy, and it made our visits a lot of fun. I didn't see her all that much, but we kept in touch through other means."

Gerald nodded and pulled into a sudden grassy flatland surrounded by mountains and a stretch of valley. "She was a friendly woman. Charlotte never had a bad word to say about anyone, at least not to me. Now she liked things done her way, but she was extremely giving. She'd loan you the shoes off her feet if you needed them." He cleared his throat and gave her a side glance. "Charlotte got on well with the Chastells, despite their contrary natures. And they loved your aunt. Burke and his brothers were always helping her with one thing or another."

"Really?" To ingratiate themselves with the old woman so she'd sell them her property?

Gerald chuckled. "Such suspicion in those pretty eyes. Really, Rachel, Charlotte loved those 'lost boys', as she liked to call them. Yes, Burke and his brothers want the land back that once belonged to them, but they never pressured Charlotte to sell. She told me that Burke had asked once, and only once. She said no, and he accepted her decision. He still put new shingles on her roof when the old ones wore down. And Grady and Dean still mow her lawn and help with odds and ends when she needs, ah, needed it."

"Grady and Dean?"

"Burke's brothers. The Chastells are three confirmed bachelors living on a large spread out here. Catamount Ranch isn't that big by ranch standards, a few hundred acres at most. And much of their land is hilly, being so near the mountains. But it's pure and clear. And it's theirs."

Like this place is now mine. Rachel rolled down her window as they pulled onto a long drive. Over a small hill a two-story, cream-colored house came into view. Warmth settled in her belly, the possibility of a new beginning taking root. Any unpleasant feeling vanished as she caught sight of her new home.

And then Burke arrived in his pick-up, kicking up dust, and shattered her peace.

Chapter Three

Burke slammed the door to his truck and ignored Rachel, scanning the surrounding forest for the uninvited signs of life he'd sensed as soon as he'd stopped the truck and took a sniff. Someone was out there, but he couldn't determine friend or foe. Too many other scents clouded the wind, though once again, Rachel's wasn't one of them. No womanly smell, no sexual need, nothing.

"Burke?"

"Why don't you show Rachel the house, Gerald? I just remembered something I forgot to take care of the last time I was here."

Gerald shot a sharp look at the woods directly beyond Burke and nodded, his nose twitching. "Good idea. Come on, Rachel. Let me show you the box Charlotte left for you. It's inside."

Rachel glanced from Gerald to Burke and nodded. To Burke's relief, she filed inside the house without a murmur of protest. His skin itching to make the change and investigate his source of unease, he walked quickly into the treeline a few hundred feet from the house and began shedding his clothing. In less than a minute, he'd stashed his clothes behind a massive boulder and shifted into his inner beast—a large mountain lion.

Breathing deep, he closed his eyes to focus, and headed west. A short distance from his starting point he saw an equally large catamount facing off against a trio of gray wolves. Didn't those bastards ever travel anywhere solo?

"*How long have they been here?*" he sent his brother Grady.

"*Too long.*" Grady hissed, scratching at the ground in front of him. One of the wolves growled, but the bigger ones by his side held him back with a small sound. The wolves eyed both cats and slowly backed away, their eyes locked until a reasonable distance had been asserted. Then they turned tail and raced into the woods.

Grady made ready to follow when Burke planted himself firmly in his path. "*No, not now. Rachel Penny, Charlotte's niece, is with Gerald in the house.*"

Eyes wide, Grady sniffed at Burke and smiled, dropping onto his belly with a grin. "*So that's why I smell sex on you. You finally used the condom, eh?*"

Burke swiped at his brother, swatting his flank with a sharp slap.

"*What the hell was that for?*" Grady glared and bared his teeth.

"*Do I really need a reason? You're a pain in the ass. How's that?*"

"*Jerk.*"

"*Bastard.*"

"*Asshole.*"

"*Nice conversation. Mind if I join in?*" Dean approached stealthily, his coat more cinnamon than his brothers', who could have been twins in their beast form. His yellow eyes gleamed with humor. "*So, Burke, you use that condom yet?*"

Grady chuffed with mirth when Burke growled at his

youngest brother.

"Not you, too. Look, Charlotte's niece is at the house with Gerald, and I need to get back before I'm missed. Grady, take care of the security around here. I take it you two still haven't found the totem?"

Dean twitched his ears in irritation. *"Except for the wolves you two just chased off, there's been nothing here since...Charlotte."* They all fell silent. *"But the niece is finally here, hmm? What's she like?"*

"She's a tough one, but I'm handling her."

"Sure you are." Grady's eyes gleamed with amusement.

"Oh ho. So that's the way of it. Was she any good?" Dean wanted to know.

Burke growled a warning before pouncing. He needed to get back to Rachel, but he'd about had it with his brothers' insinuations and teasing. Time to remind them who was in charge.

Several minutes later, he released a cursing Dean and left an amused Grady to prowl the grounds. Loping back to his clothes, he hurriedly donned them and returned to the house just as Gerald and Rachel exited.

"Ah, Burke. There you are. We were just about to come find you."

Ignoring the censure in Gerald's tone, Burke nodded at Rachel. "You okay?"

Her eyes were red-rimmed and her cheeks pale. She nodded, however, and met his gaze. "It's hard, but I'm managing. My aunt was a neat freak. So moving in should be a snap."

Burke shot a surprised glance at Gerald, who shrugged behind Rachel. "You're staying?"

Her lips thinned. "Yes. Is that going to be a problem?"

Thoughts about the totem slipped his mind as he realized Rachel staying gave him an opportunity to revisit their association from earlier this morning. He couldn't help grinning as he stared at her from head to toe. "No problem at all. I'd be more than happy to help you settle in, Rachel."

She blinked at his husky voice and took a step back in confusion. Good, he'd thrown her. Now how to lure her close again. He not only wanted to touch and taste every inch of her, but he wanted her away from this house for her own protection. And then there was that little matter of the totem's whereabouts.

Rachel coughed into her hand, breaking the sudden silence. "I, ah, I think we need to continue, Gerald. You said you'd let us know how my aunt divided the property?"

Gerald nodded at Rachel and proceeded to explain Charlotte's wishes.

Rachel gawked at Gerald, and Burke could only stare, not sure what to say. On the one hand, Charlotte's decision made it easier for him to search for the totem. And on the other... He glanced at Rachel.

"You're telling me Charlotte didn't divide the property or set up any boundaries at all." He waited for Gerald's affirmation before continuing. "So basically, my brothers and I co-own the land with Rachel, but she retains sole ownership of the actual house?"

"Ah, not exactly."

"Explain it then." Burke didn't like surprises, and Gerald's ambiguity was pissing him off big time.

"Charlotte didn't leave the land to all the Chastells. Just to you, Burke, and to Rachel." Gerald dug into his briefcase and withdrew an official envelope. "This is for you, from Charlotte.

And this one..." he paused to dig out another one, "...this one's for you, Rachel. It's supposed to explain everything. You are each to open the letters and hand them back to me when you're done." He produced a lighter. "Sorry, but she wanted me to burn the letters once you finished. Nothing says you can't share the information you read with each other, however. I didn't understand her wishes either, but per Charlotte, no one else reads your messages but you. And if you fail to abide by that minor instruction, the entire property goes to Monty GrayClaw or his descendants."

"What?"

Gerald sighed. "Just read the damned letter and burn it, Burke. It's easy enough to understand. Rachel, you okay with this?"

"Sure. I guess." She gave Burke a wary look and turned her attention back to her envelope. Opening it, she read the letter, her frown growing as her eyes flew over the page.

Burke muttered under his breath about contrary females and did the same, thinking Charlotte's grand, flowing script fit with the larger-than-life, autocratic woman who liked to boss him at every turn. Even in death she reached out to tell him what to do.

Dear Burke,

As the hotheaded leader of your pride, I expect nothing less than your very best in regards to my lovely niece, Rachel. You've been after my land for some time, and I know you only have the town's best interests at heart. To that effect, I bequeath to you the care of the totem's guardian and all that comes with her, with the exception of my house, which Rachel needs more than you can know. Of course, this is conditional on Rachel accepting you—truly accepting you.

149

She's a Penny through and through, and needs a strong man by her side. It's my deepest wish that you take her as a mate and as a wife, or if you refuse to see her coming as the gift it is, as at least a member of your pride. But make sure she fulfills her responsibilities to Cougar Falls. She was born to summon the totem. Stand by her as she learns what to do, and whatever you do, don't desert her in her time of need. Be the strong male presence in her life I never had. And don't even think of working around me on this. You're not nearly as smart as you think you are. Help my niece and help yourself. Lead her, Burke, show her the way. All or nothing. And you and the town will find a treasure to preserve the past.

Sincerely, a pain in the ass 'til the end,

Charlotte

Glancing at Gerald, Burke wondered what the hell to make of this. "You know what it says?"

Gerald nodded. "I'm the only one. You finished?" He reached for the letter, taking it from Burke's limp hand. In seconds the lighter he held burned the letter to ash, and they both turned their attention to Rachel.

Scowling, she gripped the page tighter as she finished, then reread her missive. "This is nuts." She stared at Gerald. "You actually encouraged my aunt with this nonsense?"

"It's not nonsense." Gerald nodded to the letter. "Read it again until you're sure you won't forget what's written there. I'm not allowed to assist you any more than I already have. From now on, if you have questions, Burke's here to guide you with regards to the actual property and what's in it."

Burke didn't know how the hell he was going to guide Rachel in anything considering he had no idea how to "call" the damned totem, or how to make the thing work. When

Charlotte's health had begun to fail, the totem's magic had wavered, then weakened. And when she'd died, the magic and the large relic had vanished. A twenty-foot-tall hunk of wood just...gone.

Now Charlotte implied Rachel was here to take over where she'd left off, hell, maybe even to be his wife, if Charlotte had her way, and Gerald, that asshole, had known about this the whole time.

"We've been without protection for a week." Burke took a threatening step in Gerald's direction. "If you knew, you should have—"

"I've done as I've been told. Now it's up to you and Rachel. Sink or swim, this town needs its defenses before the others step in. And I think you know who I'm talking about." Gerald stared beyond Burke toward the woods.

Yeah, Gerald had smelled the wolves as well. The encroaching bastards. The gray wolves wanted the totem for themselves, not content with their large territory in Glacier National Park. The mangy canines wanted a better handhold on "civilization", and the totem and Cougar Falls were a perfect breeding ground to start a new Order, one to rival the huge faction in Texas growing in leaps and bounds.

Rachel interrupted his chaotic thoughts. "Okay, I think I need some explanations, and I need them now."

Gerald smiled, showing too many teeth. "And that's my cue to leave." He snatched the letter from Rachel, burned it and pocketed his lighter. Grabbing his briefcase, he swiftly said his goodbyes and left them standing together, alone at last.

Rachel blinked rapidly and shook her head. "This is like some bad dream. I inherited my aunt's house with major strings attached. And what the hell is this totem, anyway? Gerald told me about a twenty-foot totem pole, but that letter said something way different. I want answers, Burke."

She planted her hands on her hips, her attitude both aggressive and scared. He wanted to know exactly what Charlotte had written, and why it made Rachel so nervous.

"Tell me what your aunt said."

"First, you tell me about this totem pole and why the town has festivals dedicated to it. And why were you fighting with mountain men just after breakfast? And while you're at it, why are most of the men I've seen in town so…"

"So what?"

"So animalistic? Not to mention loaded with testosterone and weirdly good-looking genes." She stared at him almost accusingly.

His brows rose. So did that mean she thought he was handsome as well? Even as he preened he chastised himself. *The totem, Burke. Remember the town.*

With a sigh, he grabbed his keys out of his pants pocket and tossed them in his hand. "You want the truth, is that it?" At her insistent nod, he exhaled heavily. "Fine. Maybe that'll make everything clearer. But this is going to take a while. How about you and I grab some coffee at my place? I'll behave, I promise." He wanted to smile at the small frown of disappointment curling her lips, wondering if she realized it was there. "I'll show you my neighboring land and introduce you to my idiot brothers if they're home, and then we can figure out how to work with Charlotte's last wishes so that we can both live with the results."

She cocked her head, as if weighing his sincerity. Whatever she saw satisfied her, and the tension he hadn't been aware of within him relaxed. "All right. Then you'll take me back into town to get my car?"

"Whatever you want." *So long as I get you away from rogue*

wolves and away from here. Careful not to crowd her, as much as he wanted to, he waited while she carried her box back into the house and returned after locking the front door behind her. He didn't have the heart to tell her that anyone who wanted in would find a way, if they hadn't already. Hell, he and his brothers had already looked through the home and that box, but had found nothing of any consequence, much to their dismay.

Burke helped Rachel into his truck and closed the door after her. A strange enjoyment filled him at having her to himself again, and he drove the mile separating their properties slowly.

"So what do you do on your ranch?"

He glanced at her, appreciating the glint of sunlight striking her hair into a glossy blue-black. "We raise a small herd of cattle, mostly for food, as well as a large vegetable garden. Our family's run the land for over two hundred years. We try to be self-sufficient, for the most part. But we generate much of our income from Chastell Tours, a fishing guide company Dean and Grady run. I operate the business end of it from the house." He shrugged. "I'm not one for tourists and bigger towns. What about you?"

"Well, over a year ago I split from my business partner of three years. I've been involved in legal battles since." Her lips turned down, and he saw bitterness in her gaze. "A real waste of my life." Her business partner sounded like way more than some platonic associate. "Luckily, I was always the gifted one in our partnership. I run a small business, a promotions firm that specializes in web development and management."

He nodded. "So you can do that anywhere, so long as you can get on the Internet." No reason for her to leave Cougar Falls. His blood pounded at the thought.

"Yeah. Actually, this couldn't have happened at a better time."

He glanced at her and saw her flush.

"I didn't mean that, at least, not the way it sounded. I loved Aunt Charlotte. Hell, I wish she was here right now and I was just visiting. But she's gone, and I'm at loose ends. Aunt Charlotte would have said it was fate."

Burke felt the ghostly whisper of destiny over the back of his neck. "You a big believer in fate?"

"No, actually." She chuckled and leaned her head toward the window, the wind pushing through her dark hair like threading fingers. "I don't like to think my future's planned for me. I think we all make our own destinies."

"Yeah, me too. But I've been told I have control issues."

She turned to him and her grin lit her face, a beacon of warmth he wanted to bask in. "Who told you that?"

"Grady and Dean. The two most irritating men you've ever met in your life."

"But, Burke, if they're anything like you, I can't imagine them being anything less than perfectly charming."

He laughed. "Very funny. But you'll see soon enough." He pulled into his driveway and drove the half mile to the house. A large rancher, the house had plenty of room for his pride—what used to consist of nearly twenty Shifter pairings and the occasional loner, now down to three unattached catamount males, a bear Shifter with attitude and his pretty wife. Years ago, the town suffered when the totem fell under the gray wolves' hands for a spell. Huge clan wars resulted in getting the totem back, but at a price. Many in the pride died, and the rest eventually scattered. Though saddened, his parents had said it was for the best, as many in the pride had been considering leaving anyway. Catamounts, traditionally, were solitary creatures. Typically, outside of one's immediate family, a male feline Shifter felt the urge to claim his own territory. And unlike the wolves, cats weren't pack animals; they didn't much like to share. Burke and his brothers, however, didn't fit the mold. They liked living together, with each other and with Joel and his family. They had no plans to separate, whether they mated or not.

Thoughts of mating had him glancing at Rachel, and he wondered how she would like living alone in Charlotte's house.

Rachel whistled, shifting his focus. "Holy crap, this place is huge. And so pretty."

He felt a burst of pride and parked, trying to see his house as she might. Built in sections, the main log cabin was surrounded by flowers and a small stream behind the house. Through the years, they'd added on to the house as needed, making the additions seamless. Now, thirty-four hundred square feet of space gave his pride enough room to roam without stepping all over one another, and the extra cabins near the main house gave them even more space.

"Who lives in those?" Rachel pointed to two of the six cabins visible over the hill on which the property sat.

"Joel and his wife, Maggie, live in that one. You saw them this morning in the Fox's Henhouse. Joel was the big guy sitting at the table next to mine, and Maggie was the cute blonde, his wife. She's the one who keeps the flowers so nice, while Joel works around the ranch with me. He's big into the garden."

"He's a farmer?"

"Of sorts. He loves to eat, and makes sure we have what we need to survive."

"Interesting. You sound like one of those survivalists or something."

Or something. Before he could comment further, they exited

155

the truck and were met by Dean coming off the porch. Crap.

Dean's eyes glowed with welcome, and he held out his hand with a wide grin. "Hey. Ms. Penny?"

"Word sure travels fast," she murmured to Burke before taking Dean's hand. "Call me Rachel." Dean brought her palm to his lips, and to his relief, Burke sensed no arousal wafting off the woman. But when Dean refused to let her hand go, his eyes glued to Rachel as if she were his, Burke saw red.

Possession rode him, brother or not, and he growled low in his throat, warning Dean away from what he considered his. Rachel swung to face him, her mouth open in surprise, and that quickly, the sweet scent of desire overrode the little gathering.

"*Shit.*" Dean sucked in a breath, his golden eyes glowing as he struggled not to shift, his eyes and hands caught in the change. But he didn't move away from Rachel fast enough to suit Burke.

"Mine." Burke inserted himself between her and his brother. Glaring down into Dean's gaze, he forced his brother to break away and turn fully human. Dean growled his displeasure but did as Burke bade.

"Excuse me?" Rachel's voice sounded too husky for his peace of mind.

And then Grady turned the corner and froze as the wind changed, bringing Rachel's scent to him. "So sweet," Grady rumbled and moved closer. "So rich."

"So mine," Burke said again, needing to stake his claim. Hell, he wanted to fuck Rachel right now, to more than mark her, but to mate with her, so that his brothers and every other damned male would see who she belonged to.

"Mine?" Rachel, unfortunately, didn't seem to be on the same track. "We are talking about something else and not me, aren't we?"

His brothers turned as one to stare at her, and Burke shifted on his feet, trying to will away his growing erection and regain a measure of control. "Yeah. My brothers are really into *my truck*, always trying to take what isn't theirs and isn't going to be," he tried warning more subtly.

"I'm thinking he didn't use it yet." Dean meant the condom, and just thinking about putting it on for Rachel made Burke want to howl with lust.

"Nope. This should be good." Grady grinned.

Rachel frowned. "You know, Burke, you're right. They're just as irritating as you said they'd be."

Grady and Dean laughed and stepped back, breaking some of the tension. "I like her," Grady admitted. "Stubborn, hot as hell, and she doesn't seem to like Burke much. Perfect."

Rachel blushed, her features drawn in annoyance. Burke understood all too well how she felt. He loved his brothers, but they could be such a pain sometimes. He was only three years older than Grady and five more than Dean, but at times he felt almost ancient.

"I never said I didn't like Burke. He's been very...nice to me." By her tone, he could tell she was remembering their encounter in the alley. And again his lust spiraled, his desire to mark her as feline growing almost impossible to resist.

His brothers stopped smiling as they caught the musk of intent wafting from him.

"Oh yeah," Dean whispered, his eyes again blazing. "We haven't marked a female in forever."

Rachel blinked as if in a daze, staring from Dean to Grady and then to Burke with a familiar need. Her eyes narrowed and like before, her pupils elongated. Her skin shimmered with

Shifter energy, and Burke felt the unspoken desire between them. Unfortunately, it encompassed more than just him, but his brothers as well. He didn't want to, but knowing he could right now fully mark Rachel with their help spurred his intent.

"Do you want this, Rachel?" he asked, knowing she had no idea of what he really meant. But his hormones didn't seem to care. He had to mark her in the worst way. And sexual scenting from three ready cat Shifters would certainly do the trick.

"Rachel?" Grady growled, his teeth sharp and bright under the sun.

"Rachel?" Dean repeated, licking his lips. "Just say yes."

She stared at them all, her eyes wide, her full lips parted, readying to respond. Burke scented arousal, confusion, and the first stirrings of feminine fear, bringing him fast to the point of no return. He could fight against arousal, but the smell of fear stirred his need to hunt. And taking Rachel was something he wanted more than his next breath.

The sound of a vehicle approached, tearing Rachel's attention. Like a switch that had been thrown, the smell of her arousal abruptly disappeared, leaving three highly aroused Shifters nowhere to go but frustrationville.

Chapter Four

Rachel swayed as she stared at the familiar blonde coming toward her with a bright smile. Dizzy, she could only breathe deeply and blink to clear her blurred vision. Dean and Grady spun and left without another word, and their departure made her upset for some reason. She'd been wanting something...

But it was Burke who drew and held her attention from the blonde. His hair blew around his face despite the calm, and his amber eyes looked overly bright in such a harsh, masculine face. His mouth was taut, as if Burke strained against hunger. Enthralled by the sharp sight of him, her gaze wandered from his eyes to his long throat to his broad chest and farther down, finally resting on the large bulge tense against the front of his jeans.

Confusion filled her. Burke wanted her, of that she had no doubt. And the others...they'd been, what? Aroused and wanting her too? A woman his brothers had just met? They couldn't possibly have intimated they'd desired her. That nonsense about marking? She tore her gaze from his erection and stared into his needy eyes. The look on Burke's face just now. None of it made any sense.

He stepped closer and wrapped his arms around her.

"Burke?"

He deliberately tightened his hold, as if to show her who was in charge. But before she could protest, he kissed her. Hard, possessive lips ravaged her mouth. He speared her with his tongue, the flavor of him knocking her for a loop. Had Burke not held her, she would surely have fallen. Her tongue met his and slipped into his mouth, pulling a hoarse groan from him. She felt his erection burning against her belly, and that spiral of heat that seemed to come and go whenever he neared flared again. God, she wanted so much to feel him inside of her.

She pressed against him, nearly climbing him to get closer, but as she moved her lips over his something scratched her mouth.

Burke froze and tore his mouth from hers. His eyes were that eerie golden color, the shape of his pupils resembling that of a cat. He stared at the bottom of her lip, which stung, and leaned down to kiss her, gently this time. He shuddered and ran his tongue over her lower lip before thrusting her as far from him as he could.

"Maggie, help Rachel to a cup of coffee, would you?" She loved his voice, so deep and rough, and so sexy she wanted to melt. Then the name "Maggie" registered. Who was he talking to? "I'll be right back."

Burke left in a blur, and once again Rachel felt reality slipping from her. When she could focus again, she found herself sitting in a chair in a masculine but homey kitchen. A petite blonde, probably Maggie, was whistling and shuttling from cabinet to cabinet.

"Damn. Those guys never refill from the larder."

"Larder?" Was that croak Rachel's voice?

"Wait here, hon. I'll be right back. Out of coffee, and of course nobody but me refills the damned jar." She walked out of the kitchen before Rachel could say anything else, leaving

Rachel alone with her thoughts for the first time since reading her aunt's startling letter.

Impressions of Burke lingered, but she couldn't make sense of the odd episode with him and his brothers. Since trying to recall details of that strange meeting gave her a headache, Rachel's concentration shifted to the information her aunt had imparted in that letter, and Rachel wondered if she could even believe half of it.

According to Aunt Charlotte, Rachel was more needed in Cougar Falls than she knew. The task of watching over the precious totem all these people seemed so fixated on was a Penny tradition. For some odd reason, Charlotte believed only she, and people of her blood, could see and locate the totem as its true guardians. And if Rachel chose to believe that nonsense, then she had to also believe what her aunt said about her neighbors—that the Chastells were said protectors of this mystical totem.

Per Charlotte's instructions, the best things for Rachel to do, in order of importance, were one: to be thankful for finally ridding herself of that leech Jesse Minton and celebrate with a good case of wild, passionate sex with a man like Burke Chastell; two: convince the same Burke Chastell to marry her, because a more perfect match couldn't have been made in heaven; and three: find the totem with Burke, and quickly, so that the town didn't fall apart in Charlotte's absence. *Follow your heart*, Charlotte had written, emphasizing the "follow".

As if that information weren't startling enough, Charlotte also had several suggestions pertaining to the choosing of Rachel's inner beast, whichever creature on the totem that appealed to her more than the others. Charlotte speculated that Rachel would probably choose the puma, but then again, the fox had always intrigued Charlotte, so who knew?

What the hell had her aunt been smoking up here? Had the letter been written in some kind of code? Rachel had wanted to better examine it, but good old Gerald hadn't given her a chance. He'd torched the thing in seconds, leaving her with more questions than answers. Shifters, totems, and hot sex that wasn't even sex, really, with a guy she'd just met and didn't exactly like in an alleyway?

Okay, she could scratch the part about not liking Burke. Despite her mistrust, she couldn't help her attraction to the man. And the more she thought about it, the more she realized their intimacy in the alley had been anything but staged. The passion that flared between them was too damned real, and she'd seen Burke's confusion as well as his attraction on the three occasions the heat had risen between them.

Burke was actually kind of nice, in a sexy, totally masculine, tough-guy way. She liked the fact that he had responsibilities, that his brothers annoyed him and that her aunt apparently thought enough of him to recommend him for marriage. Not to mention he'd given her a mother of an orgasm through her freaking *clothes*. She could only imagine what he'd feel like without anything between them...

Flushing and shaking free of *those* thoughts, she tried to make sense of her aunt's allusions to inner beasts and that totem. Which had her reexamining Burke's glimpses of weirdness. In that alley he'd been wild, both with those hairy guys and with her. And just now... In her mind's eye, she saw him and his brothers again, the three of them staring at her with cat-like pupils and shimmery skin. Her breath caught. She really had seen that, hadn't she? And if so, did that mean Charlotte was right about the rest of it? Could Rachel become one of them—whatever "them" meant?

"Found it."

Maggie's voice shocked Rachel into a sudden jerk that nearly threw her out of her chair.

"Oh, I'm sorry. I didn't mean to startle you. I found the coffee." The petite blonde prepared the pot and took two ceramic mugs from a cabinet, placing one in front of Rachel and the other in front of her seat across the table. "I'm Maggie Buchanan, Joel's wife. We live here with Burke and his brothers, tending the ranch."

"Yeah. Burke mentioned you."

Maggie beamed. "He's a wonderful man, isn't he? A bit too high-handed at times, but the men around here tend to be real throw-backs, you know what I mean? It's all that mountain air, I think." She winked at Rachel. "But they sure do know how to kiss, don't they?"

Rachel blushed, recalling the whopper Burke had planted on her right in front of Maggie. Rachel stared at the smaller woman, aware of the normalcy Maggie projected. She seemed extremely nice and accepting, harmless really. Maybe she could shed some light on what was truly going on around here.

"How long have you lived here?"

"All my life." Maggie grinned. "I love Cougar Falls. I met Joel seven years ago when he moved back into town. He stayed and we fell in love. We're coming up on our fifth anniversary next month."

"Congratulations." Rachel paused, trying to find a way to frame her next question. "So did you know my aunt too?"

"Sure did. Charlotte was a great friend, and a funny lady. She bossed your brothers something fierce." Maggie chuckled. "I loved seeing them run ragged after a day with Charlotte. They'd bitch about it with Joel, but always with a grin. She treated them like family, and they've missed that. Their parents died years ago, back when Burke was just eighteen. He's been

163

raising his brothers and managing this place himself for a long time." Maggie rose when the coffee machine beeped and brought to the table a carafe, a container of milk and one of sugar. She gave Rachel a speculative look. "What about you?"

"Me?" Rachel busied herself by fixing her coffee.

"Do you have family to get back to? A husband and some kids, maybe?" Maggie stared at Rachel's fingers wrapped around her mug.

"No. No husband, not anymore." Her relief in saying that made her smile.

"A real jerk, huh?"

"You have no idea."

"Well, I'm glad you're rid of him then. Had a boyfriend a while back who wasn't so nice to me." Maggie's voice softened. "Took me a while to see the light. That and Joel." Her face brightened. "I didn't want to give Joel the time of day, but he wore me down. And I'm glad he did. I'd do anything for that man."

Rachel wondered what it would be like to have a man she could love as much as Maggie seemed to love Joel. Even with Jesse she'd been somewhat remote, walling off that part of herself he'd never quite reached. Sex with him had been great, but now she had to wonder, had she ever talked about him the way Maggie talked about Joel? Had she ever had that glow in her eyes thinking about her ex?

"So what do you think of the town so far?"

Rachel zeroed in on the question, pleased to turn away uncomfortable thoughts about her ex, as well as to take the opportunity to question Maggie about Cougar Falls. "It's cute, but a little odd."

"You think?" Was that humor behind Maggie's bland

words?

"What do you know about this totem pole everyone celebrates? My aunt seemed to think it held magical properties. And that she was responsible for it."

"She was."

Rachel stared, pleased but cautious at Maggie's honesty. "In what way?"

"Look, Rachel, if I hadn't been born and raised here, I wouldn't believe half the things I've heard, let alone seen. Believe what you feel. Charlotte did. Suffice it to say your aunt was a well-respected and very important woman in this town. Her blood—your blood—runs as far back as the Salish who used to live here hundreds of years ago. And that totem is a symbol of everything Cougar Falls represents. Now that it's missing, a lot of people are hoping you'll bring it back."

Great. So whatever Aunt Charlotte had been smoking, Maggie had taken a few puffs of it too.

"Sounds nutty, I know. And that's just the tip of the iceberg."

Rachel was about to ask her about the Ac-taw and inner beasts when Burke and a giant of a man joined them.

"Maggie, time to gather the veggies." The giant nodded at Rachel, his dark brown eyes tender as they fell on his wife, and Rachel placed him as a man she'd seen in the diner.

"That's my husband, Joel, my own grizzly bear." Joel frowned at Maggie's laugh and hauled her out of the kitchen. "See you later, Rachel," she yelled over her shoulder, leaving Rachel alone with Burke.

He studied her with very normal, though very handsome, whiskey-brown eyes. Burke moved with grace, grabbing a mug and joining her at the table without taking his eyes off of her.

His stare made her nervous…and made her hot.

"What?"

"You are the damnedest woman."

She didn't know how to take that.

"You've been hit with a street fight, a touchy-feely stranger in an alley," he said, self-deprecatingly. "Then there's your aunt's will, and the crazy shit I'm sure she wrote about, and not the least my brothers. I thought by now you'd be running for the airport."

"I would, but I need my car." She relaxed, flattered truth be told, that he seemed to both like and respect her.

He chuckled. "I can see a lot of Charlotte in you. And that's a good thing, in case you're wondering." He poured himself some coffee and drank it black, smiling at her over the brim.

"Burke," Rachel started, not wanting to lose this easy discourse between them but needing to have it said. "My aunt said some strange things in her letter."

"I can imagine."

"You said you'd do your best to explain things to me. How about you start?"

"Ah, a tall order." He took another swallow and his hair swung down into his eyes. Without thinking about it, she leaned forward and pushed it back, startling him and herself.

"Sorry."

"I'm not. I like you touching me." He took a deep breath and closed his eyes. When he opened them again, he didn't look happy. "I'm going to tell you the truth. And you're going to think I'm one hundred percent certifiable. But do me a favor and listen until I'm done, okay? I can prove what I'm going to tell you. Just hear me out."

Rachel nodded, her pulse racing.

"Cougar Falls isn't like any town you've ever been to, Rachel. The people who live here were either born here or married into one of the founding families. I was born here with my brothers, like my parents and their parents before them. We're Ac-taw."

She processed what he said, her eyes wide. "Animal souls? You're a part of those people the Salish first found?" At his surprise, she explained, "Gerald filled me in on the Totem Festival on the drive over. That and a bit more."

"Yeah. Truth is, most of the town is Ac-taw. And the totem is the real deal, passed down for generations. Charlotte preserved it for us, and we protected her."

Rachel frowned. "From what?"

"From those Shifters who would take it from us."

"Shifters?"

"Humans can't find Cougar Falls. It's not on any map, and doesn't 'exist' to outsiders."

For the moment ignoring "humans", Rachel asked, "Then why could I find it? I'm not Ac-taw."

"Actually, you are. Charlotte was too, at least distantly. That's why she was so in tune with the totem and the world around her. To many, she was a nutcase," he said bluntly. "But she was so much more than that. She was a spirit guide, a guardian of the magic in the totem. And when she died, she took the knowledge of the totem with her. The town needs it back. We need you, Rachel, to get it back for us."

Rachel shook her head. "I have no idea what you're talking about. I mean, I read my aunt's letter. I know she believed what you do. But I don't know anything about this totem or how to get it back. It wasn't in the house or anywhere around the property that I could see. And there was nothing about it in the box Gerald showed me."

167

"The knowledge is within you." Burke touched his heart. "Once you open yourself to the beast within—"

"About this beast. My aunt seems to think I can choose my 'inner beast', whatever the hell that is. Care to explain?"

Burke sighed. "Why don't I show you instead?" He whistled and in moments, Dean and Grady appeared in the doorway. Though she hadn't seen them pass the window, they must have been waiting nearby. "Grady? How about you do the honors? Show Rachel your animal soul."

Grady's eyes lit up with approval. "Don't freak, Rachel. This is totally normal." He began removing his clothes, much to her surprise and admitted appreciation. The Chastells were enough to make any woman's heart race. A glance at Dean showed him leaning against the doorframe, his gaze glued to her. Burke sat beside her scowling, but said nothing more.

"Why would I freak, Grady?" She couldn't believe he was actually stripping down to nothing but golden skin. God, Grady was just as big and almost as gorgeous as Burke. "There's a handsome man getting naked in front of me and his brothers. I keep thinking I should be giving you money or something. How about some music to add to the mood?"

Dean chuckled, and even Burke choked on a laugh.

She had mere moments to see Grady naked, however, because as soon as he shucked his underwear he went down on all fours, and she had to lean over the table to watch. He seemed to shimmer, his tanned flesh growing brighter and then softer as skin became fur, joints realigned and a tail formed. His eyes, as they stared at her, turned a brighter gold, the pupils slitted in what appeared to be a cat-like face. It seemed to take forever, but in mere seconds Grady had disappeared, replaced by a mature male cougar.

Rachel forgot to breathe as she stared at a freaking *cat*

person, one of her aunt's favorite Shifters in the many tales she liked to share. Rachel didn't know what to say, and could scarcely believe what she was seeing.

"He's real," Burke said softly. "Go ahead and touch him. He won't bite."

Rachel stood slowly and walked around the table to...Grady? His tail swooshed along the floor where he sat waiting, his eyes unblinking. She glanced again to Burke, afraid and excited and disbelieving all at once.

Burke pushed back his chair and crouched with her in front of Grady. He lifted her hand and placed it on Grady's head. "Go ahead, honey. Feel him. It's Grady in there. We're feline Shifters, catamounts. Better known as cougars or pumas." He pressed his warm hand over hers, pushing her fingers along Grady's soft coat.

"Oh my God." She stared at their hands, then at Grady's half-closed eyes. When he began to purr, her gaze shot back to Burke. "You did that. After...when we...at the alley. You purred."

"I did." Burke caressed her hand before letting go. "I was very content."

His sexy drawl gained her body's immediate response, and Grady tensed under her hand. She immediately stilled, unnerved when Dean approached and stood behind her, boxing her in.

"You see, Rachel, it's like this," Burke began, licking his lips as he stared at her. "You and Charlotte are a lot alike. Neither of you cast a scent. Or at least, you don't unless you're aroused. And at least three times since you've been here you've set me off like a rocket. You accused me of taking advantage of you in that alley to get Charlotte's land. Honey, I hate to break it to you, but I'm helpless when you're turned on."

Grady nodded, an odd sight, seeing a big cat nod in agreement.

"We all are," Dean added. "It's been so long since we've had a female feline."

Rachel swallowed around a dry throat. All this talk of turning her on was doing just that. Grady pushed his head under her hand, forcing her to stroke between his ears and under his chin.

"Cut it out." Burke pushed his huge head away. "Quit rubbing all over her. She's mi—" He broke off just as he glanced back at her. "Sorry. Grady can get a tad possessive."

Behind her Dean snorted.

"What did you mean before when you talked about marking a female?" She wanted to know, as much as she didn't want to know.

Dean answered. "Marking a female means you accept her as one of your own, as part of a pride or clan, a family unit. Shifters are born, not made. So marking is very, very rare. But every now and then, an Ac-taw like you comes around. A person who can choose her beast."

"My inner beast," Rachel said, remembering her aunt's words.

"Yes. That inner beast is your animal soul calling out to you. That you can choose from any you encounter speaks to your power over the totem. That and the fact you project no scent. You're a very powerful woman, Rachel. And we would be honored to mark you as ours."

She couldn't explain the rush she felt hearing that, but she still didn't understand. "As yours? What exactly does that mean?" Had they marked Maggie, too? But Maggie was married to Joel, so maybe it wasn't a sexual thing.

Burke helped her to her feet and settled her back in her chair. She watched in awe as Grady stretched and changed back, then dressed again.

"A mark is a sign of belonging." Dean sat next to her. "We—" he paused to motion to his brothers, "—are each marked as part of this pride, a group of Shifters led by catamounts. Joel and Maggie are marked as ours too, though they're not cats. Marking isn't the same as mating or joining."

"Huh?"

Burke shook his head. "Dean, you're making a muck of it. Let me explain." He turned to Rachel. "A mark is a subtle scent other Shifters can smell. It lets everyone know who's loyal to whom. Though in Cougar Falls, all the clans pretty much have an affinity to the town. Our pride is the most diverse, because we don't care what breed of Shifter we accept.

"We mark by scent in a variety of ways. We marked Maggie and Joel over time, allowing small measures of our hormones to cover them. Completely painless and nonsexual, I promise you."

"As if I'd make it with a bear," Dean muttered.

"Bear?" Rachel's mind felt sluggish. "But Maggie's so small."

"No. Maggie's mostly human. Maggie has a touch of Ac-taw still in her that lets her see Cougar Falls when others can't. Joel's the bear."

"Okay." It was starting to make an odd kind of sense. Rachel stared at Grady, still trying to place him on the floor with whiskers and large teeth. He winked at her.

"Marking can be sexually done, but it doesn't have to be. Joining is sex, pure and simple." Burke stared hard at her and cleared his throat. "And then there's mating."

"As in Shifter marriage," Grady explained. "It's permanent

and very spiritual. And the sex is to die for, or so I've heard." His gaze wandered over her body suggestively, lingering on her breasts.

Rachel crossed her arms over her chest defensively, trying to protect her body from Grady, as well as her lust from growing out of control around the dangerous Chastells. Burke apparently read her discomfort because he shoved a hard elbow into Grady's gut. Grady flashed long sharp teeth in what sounded like a hiss, but before they could distract her, Rachel pressed for more information.

"So you guys wanted to mark me? Why?"

Burke looked pained by the conversation but he answered her. "You haven't chosen an animal soul yet, Rachel. And you're so feline, it's killing me. We would have you as one of us, to strengthen our clan."

"And because you're hot as hell," Dean offered.

"Shut up, Dean." Grady growled, rubbing his belly.

Rachel didn't know what to think. "So, ah, there are other Shifter 'clans', is that the right word?"

"Yeah. You met two of the silver fox clan today, Gerald and Ty, the sheriff. We have bears, catamounts—us—some eagle and raptor clans. And then there are the wolves." The way Burke said "wolves" she knew they weren't particularly well liked. "I fought a few of them in the alley earlier. And there've been wolves prowling around your place looking for the totem the past two weeks."

"What?" Those hairy thugs were wolves? Funny, she'd have thought they'd look more polished and graceful.

"Yeah. The gray wolves really want to start a breeding town here. To that end, they used to pressure Charlotte a lot when she first moved here. My parents held them off, then we did when we took over." Burke looked uncomfortable but he maintained eye contact. "Rachel, we did want, and still do, the land back that Charlotte owned. It was in our family for years before one of our idiot relatives lost it in a bet. But we'd never do anything to force you to sell. We kind of liked Charlotte near us. And we take pride in the fact that we were her protectors."

"Just like we're now your protectors," Grady added quietly.

She felt their stares and glanced at Burke helplessly. He wasn't the bad guy she'd first thought. He was a bona fide myth walking on two legs, or was that four, who wanted to protect her. Good Lord. What should she do about that?

"I want to help." And she did. She hadn't seen much, but she trusted what she'd seen, and she listened to her instincts. They hadn't failed her yet, and had she heeded them in the first place, she never would have married Jesse... Funny, but thoughts of him after what she'd seen didn't matter much anymore.

"And we want to help you. What can we do, Rachel?"

She shrugged. "I don't know. My aunt didn't tell me anything useful about the totem."

"What did she say, exactly?" Burke asked.

Rachel flushed, distinctly remembering her aunt's thoughts about what to do with Burke. "She told me to forget about my loser ex-husband, to find my inner beast, and ..."

"And?" Burke's gaze intensified.

"And to take my responsibility for the totem seriously." As if she was going to tell him her aunt wanted them to marry after hot, wild sex. Embarrassing.

"Right." Did Burke sound disappointed?

"What did she tell you?"

"To protect you and to help you in any way that I can."

"So how do we do that?"

Grady held up a hand. "I think we should start with Rachel's beast. You need to get in touch with yourself first. Charlotte was always preaching that to me."

"Yeah. So." Dean paused. "You want us to mark you now or later? Maybe some lunch first for strength?"

"Dean." Burke rolled his eyes. "Give her some room to breathe, okay? Rachel, it's a lot to digest. How about we go for a walk and I'll show you around? You can see Charlotte's, I mean, your house from on top of the hill near the eastern cabins."

Rachel nodded and stood. "Some air would be nice." Looking at Grady and Dean, she clearly read their disappointment. But honestly, she didn't know what to think about what she'd been told. Marking? Mating? Ac-taw that were real? And why couldn't she stop thinking about what Burke would look like when he shifted? About how hard his muscles would be under her palm before his skin turned to fur?

Burke couldn't help a quiet sigh of regret that Rachel hadn't taken Dean up on his offer to mark her. Though her scent was tamped, his arousal kept building the longer he was around her. She just kept getting prettier every time he looked at her.

She'd taken their news well, so far that he could tell. The only glitch on this morning was the knowledge she'd been married. He'd bet the ranch her ex was the business partner she'd spoken of with bitterness. Some asshole who didn't appreciate a woman like Rachel didn't deserve her.

They walked outside along the spring, the deep grasses, wild flowers and honeybees a symphony of nature that couldn't compare to Rachel's feminine beauty.

"So you were married huh?" *Dumb, Burke. Real dumb.*

She frowned but nodded. "Three years. He cheated on me, I

left, and he tried to bilk me out of our joint business assets and every dollar I'd broken my back to earn."

"What a dick."

She blinked at him and smiled, a genuine grin that made his heart pound with desire. "Truer words were never spoken." They walked in silence a few moments before she said, "How about you? Ever married? Been heavily involved? It wasn't Sarah Duncan was it?"

"Hell no." Horrified at the thought, he caught her nasty chuckle. "Funny. No, it wasn't Sarah. You blasted me for talking down to her, and maybe I deserved it. But that woman will not take no for an answer. She's been bugging me for years."

Rachel stared. "No kidding."

He flushed, feeling stupid. "I like sex. It's just that for me, it has to be with a person I care about." *So why did you take Rachel up against a wall? A woman you'd just met?* He quickly hurried the topic. "I've never been married. Never found a woman I wanted to commit to. We Chastells marry for life. No infidelity, no divorce. Sounds corny, but we marry for love. Always have. And hopefully always will."

"That sounds lovely." Her voice was thick, and when he turned to her, he saw tears in her eyes. "I should have waited. Every instinct told me Jesse was wrong for me. Even Aunt Charlotte told me to forget about him. But I was lonely. My parents had just died and I felt so lost."

He put an arm around her shoulders and they walked beside the stream. Being with her felt so right, as if he'd found the other half of himself long missing.

"I felt the same way when my parents died. Hell, they'd survived clan wars and a rash of poachers. Even land developers who made a real nuisance of themselves before I was born. And then they died in a stupid plane wreck."

She squeezed his hand by her shoulder, and he squeezed back.

"I still miss the hell out of them," he admitted. "Raising Grady and Dean through high school was a bitch, as I'm sure you can imagine." He met her laughing gaze. "And the holidays are never the same. But I guess unlike you, I went in the other direction. Instead of looking for someone, I kind of hid back here at the ranch. I mean, who wants to find love when it can leave you in an instant?"

As soon as he said it, he realized he spoke the truth...and that he sounded like a complete, emotional asswipe.

Embarrassed, he turned her attention to an eagle cresting in the distance. But her touch on his face startled him into turning back to her.

"Burke?"

"Yeah?"

"Thanks." The kiss she gave him was nothing like anything he'd ever experienced. Full of promise, tenderness and affection, it pulled him deeper into the quagmire of emotion he didn't want to feel for this woman, yet was helpless to deny.

Chapter Five

Rachel swore as she sneezed again. Damn, Aunt Charlotte might have dusted the attic at least once every ten years.

For the past week and a half, Rachel had spent every morning with Burke trying to figure out how to find the totem and every evening sifting through more of Charlotte's stuff. Moving in had been easy. Rachel had no furniture, just a bunch of clothes and toiletries she'd brought with her. She still rented a small storage facility back in Chicago full of books and odds and ends from her prior life.

As much as she regretted some things she'd done, Rachel didn't regret a single minute spent in Cougar Falls. She absolutely loved the town. Though she'd returned her rental car to the airport and knew she needed to find her own transportation, she'd found it easier to ride into town with Burke when he stopped by, which was at least three times a day. She couldn't help the jolt of lust, and what felt like growing affection, every time she saw him.

Thoughts of Jesse paled next to remembrances of Burke. Rachel could drown in Burke's eyes, and never got tired of his broad, sexy grin. Much as she'd tried to forget it, she could still feel him pounding against her in that alleyway as if it had just happened. And several times she'd felt on fire, as if she'd die if he didn't make love to her. Fortunately, she'd been in bed during those instances, and she'd taken care of the problem herself. She flushed, recalling how often she'd had to do that during her brief marriage. Another sign Jesse hadn't been "The One".

She had no doubt, however, that life with Burke would be nothing so tame. A man like Burke would want sex often, and he'd want it hot.

Shit. Again with the libido. She fanned her chest and then said to hell with it. She was alone and in her home. The sun had set. Who would see her up in her aunt's windowless attic? Shrugging out of her oppressive shirt, she continued to clean the attic, looking for any sign of instruction pertaining to the totem.

During the past week, she'd learned more from Burke and his brothers, and Gerald as well. Though, as the lawyer had stated, he refused to answer any questions she had about the totem, he told her a lot about the town and its inhabitants. Gerald was a silver fox Shifter. A "wily bastard", as Burke often pointed out, and a ladies' man. Gerald had been a perfect gentleman with her, however. Maybe due to the hissing and rumbled warnings Burke sent the man anytime they ran into him.

Dean and Grady still voiced their worries that she'd choose another clan to bond with. And they made it plain they wanted *her*. Maybe it was a power thing with the totem. Yet the looks they gave her, the ones that spoke of carnal hungers they'd love to assuage, made her wonder just what kind of sexual practices the catamounts observed.

Burke seemed the possessive type, but she remembered the sexual vibes coming off of him and his brothers that day at his house. She shivered at the thought. Three men who looked like the Chastells and Rachel? *Wow.* She could just imagine taking them all on, and had used the inspiration to cool her jets a time or two.

The temperature rose and she shed her jeans. Though it had to be around fifty outside, the attic sweltered. Thoughts of sex with the Chastells didn't help any either, and she told herself to flat-out stop it. *Focus, Rachel. Sex is not one of your priorities right now.* She couldn't help her wicked conscience that added*, But it should be.*

Taking a deep breath, Rachel stood and crossed her arms over her chest, staring around her. "Okay, Aunt Charlotte, help me out here. How do I find your totem and take care of Cougar Falls?"

Several times during her visits into town she'd seen more of the hairy, unkempt wolf clan loitering around. They threatened with just their presence, and they always seemed to be near when she walked anywhere. Gerald had noticed just today and remarked on the fact. But she refused to say anything to Burke, afraid he'd stop taking her into town. And come on, not being able to sample any of Millie's ice cream was just plain cruel.

She felt Burke's urgency daily, and wanted to find the totem as much for the town as for him. According to Burke, the magic in the relic would keep the wolves away, and those "pesky humans". How the heck a piece of old wood could hide an entire town from society she didn't know. But she didn't understand shifting either, and she'd seen it with her own two eyes.

Sighing, she looked behind several boxes, glad she'd batted down the cobwebs and dust balls earlier. Rachel found a box tucked behind an old mirror she hadn't previously seen and dusted the grime off the top. The cardboard ripped as she opened it, and she stared inside at old pictures. Interesting stuff, but not now, not when she had a mission to fulfill. If only that damned totem would turn up. No one had seen it anywhere on Charlotte's property. It had just vanished from its position in a shaded glen when Charlotte passed away. Very, very strange. And her aunt had ordered Burke to help Rachel find the thing.

Honestly, how could Burke guide her to find the missing totem when he had no idea where to look? No passwords, no maps, just Charlotte's frustrating letter telling Rachel to *"trust yourself, look deep into your heart and follow your beast, for he'll show you the way"*.

So did that mean she had to choose an animal soul to find the blasted totem? Because it sure was looking that way. She'd taken Grady's demonstration as truth and had peppered Burke, his brothers and Gerald for information about the clans. Bear, cougar, eagle, raptor, wolf and fox Shifters all lived together in Cougar Falls. The majority of the town seemed to consist of the fox and eagle clans, followed closely by the bears and raptors. Not so many wolves, though the few that Burke had pointed out looked nothing like their hairy brethren from Glacier Park.

She thought perhaps that was why Burke and his brothers wanted her, seeing as how few catamount Shifters there were. Burke said that many of the cats had died during clan wars, when the totem went missing a long time ago. The rest had left in the years since, striking out to claim their own territories. But Burke insisted he and his brothers had no plans to leave. Catamounts were loners, but the Chastells definitely weren't, nor were the members in their pride. Though the Ac-taw held animal souls, they also lived as humans. And they loved and laughed with one another, needing the close companionship their kind brought. Which was what made Cougar Falls such a remarkable place. Shifters of all clans were welcome, and they lived together to form a solid unit. Though Burke was a catamount, he protected the totem. Sheriff Tyler Roderick was a silver fox, as was Gerald, but the two worked so that the law would function. Joel was a bear, Millie a raptor, and yet they both served the town in different ways.

Rachel nodded to herself and shoved the box of pictures to the side. She needed to serve a purpose in this town too, and not just to contribute to the local economy. Her Internet had been connected yesterday, and her business was ready to roll as soon as she fixed the totem problem. Money wouldn't be a concern for quite a while thanks to Aunt Charlotte's generosity, and anything else she might need Burke had already offered to give her. He, Grady and Dean had done a thorough inspection on the house the day she'd moved in, fixing the hot water heater and the leaky faucet in the upstairs bathroom.

Burke had also insisted on a state of the art security system that he'd paid for himself, to her chagrin. It wasn't that she didn't appreciate it, but she didn't want to feel beholden to him. She wanted them on equal footing when they... When they what?

She groaned at the sudden image of them entwined, naked, on her bed. Rachel just couldn't stop fantasizing about having real sex with Burke, and she didn't know what to think. Ever since that walk by the stream she'd softened toward him, having found a kindred spirit of sorts. She loved how he'd shared his feelings, then been totally embarrassed by doing so. It made him so *human*, so down-to-earth approachable for a man who looked as handsome as he did. And it also showed how completely different he was from Jesse.

Jesse would have taken Sarah Duncan up on her offer for sex in a heartbeat. Jesse would never have offered to fix Millie's car or taken Rachel into town whenever she needed something with no strings attached. Burke wanted to find the totem, yes, but more, he seemed to like spending time with *Rachel*. They'd caught a movie, played spades with his cheating brothers, and watched the sun set last night, sitting together on a picnic blanket behind his house holding hands. And Burke always made sure either he, Grady or Dean were around to chase off the encroaching wolves near her property.

No, Jesse would never have lifted a finger to help her with anything that didn't get him something in return. He wasn't even half the man, or cat, she thought with a grin, that Burke was. Jesse was...

"A man I no longer need to think about with anything but pity." She grinned at the notion, realizing she was finally over the jerk. It had taken nine months of wrangling, and three more months of sour grapes, but she felt free. *At last.*

Nearly skipping out of the attic and down the stairs toward the bedroom, she didn't see the tall figure waiting for her in the landing and shrieked when strong arms closed around her.

"Shh, it's okay, Rachel. It's me, Burke."

She sagged in his hold for a moment, her heart racing out of her chest. And then she squirmed to push him away, punching him in the chest. "What the hell are you doing in here? You scared me half to death!"

"Sorry, but you didn't answer when I knocked. And I got...worried." His low voice grew lower, his eyelids shuttered as he stared at her.

Rachel was suddenly aware she'd left her clothes in the attic, and now stood before Burke in a lacy pink bra and panties.

"Fuck me," he groaned, breathing heavily. His eyes flashed and his fingers curled. "Rachel, you're killing me, you know that?"

Need, sure and true, suddenly filled her. And she wanted nothing more than to feel him inside of her. *I'm free*, she reminded herself. *Free to do what feels good. And Burke feels like heaven whenever I'm near.*

"*Have wild and passionate sex,*" Aunt Charlotte had written. Yeah, that sounded just right. "Burke, are you doing this to me?"

"Doing what?" His voice was thick as he took a step to close the distance between them.

"Making me hot. I burn," she said, nearly panting. "I want you so much I can't see straight." He licked his lips, and she saw one large canine before he closed his mouth again. The sight stirred her, making her want more.

"I don't know why, but you're flashing in and out of heat. I felt it that day in the alley, and later at my house. Baby, if you don't want this, tell me now. Because I'm about to seriously lose it if I'm not inside you in like the next thirty seconds."

"But I'm all dirty."

"Good, I like dirty." Burke ripped his shirt off, heedless of the scattering buttons. He reached for his pants but Rachel stopped him. Burke froze, completely still.

God, how she'd dreamed of this. "No. Let me." Rachel slowly popped open his jeans and slid the zipper over his thick erection. Her hands brushed his fly and he trembled, his eyes glowing and locked on her. The zipper seemed to go on forever, but when it stopped she caught her breath. Beneath his jeans Burke wore nothing, and she could see his shaft hard and flushed in a bed of dark hair.

Reaching inside, she couldn't quite close her fist around his cock, and she groaned with him at the feel of their flesh touching.

"I want to come inside you, not in your damn hand," Burke growled, completely feral. "Take me out, baby, now."

She pushed his jeans down and he kicked out of his boots and pants and stripped off his socks. Completely nude, he looked like sex incarnate. A broad chest and ropy biceps, a ripped abdomen, hard muscle over sun-darkened skin, and that potent erection straining toward her. God, his thighs, his ass... Rachel drenched her panties just looking at him. And then that scent wafted over her, that sweet, sexy smell of need and cat and Burke.

Stripping out of her bra and panties, she trembled as Burke's gaze traced every movement, his attention keen, like a predator intent on prey. He rumbled deep in his chest, his purring loud and enticing as he stalked closer.

"I'm going to make you scream. I'm going to take you the way I should have that first time, hard and rough, and I'm going to come inside you. My seed bathing your womb."

Oh shit, he was really turning her on. A small sense of preservation had her mumbling about a condom, but Burke cut her off, his scent drenching her with need. Suddenly she couldn't find it in her to care, hazy with desire. She muffled that inner voice screaming for caution, and gave way to the beast within her wanting to join with another, stronger partner.

His kiss ravaged her senses. "No condom, no birth control. We're both clean. I want this with you. You're mine, Rachel. *Mine.*" He snarled and braced her against the wall in the hallway, repeating their experience in the alley. But this time they were both naked, and the feel of his sleek chest against her breasts, of his cock brushing her moist curls, had her arching into him.

"Burke. I want you so much."

"Yeah, hard and fast." He panted and spread her thighs, holding her hips as he aligned with her wet sex. In one sharp thrust, he impaled her, the feel of his immense girth both painful and ecstatic.

"More," she gasped before he sealed her mouth with his. His tongue shot between her lips as he began fucking her, taking her with force against the wall. His scent settled deep into her bones, the feel of him more than physical, but like a brand that had staked a permanent claim. Her nails lengthened and she scratched at his back as she took his pounding, reveling in his vigor. And still it wasn't enough. She needed to feel him spurt inside of her, to smell his seed overtaking her womb.

"Burke," she screamed, her voice pitched high, her cry not her own.

He grunted and continued to thrust, his cock huge, his hands prying her ass cheeks apart as he toyed with her rim and pushed a finger past it.

She stiffened as sensation overwhelmed her. His pubic bone brushed her clit. His shaft pushed her G-spot again and again while his finger pressured nerves inside her ass. The steady friction of his chest against her aching nipples multiplied the eroticism of his mouth as his tongue stabbed her in time with his cock's thrusts... She was so close, just within reach, and then he bit her neck, sucking hard as moisture trickled from the wound. Rachel clung to him as she shattered, clenching him tight as her inner walls sucked his cock deep.

"Bite me," he rasped as he continued to plunge, and lost in the haze of his making, she settled her mouth over the juncture between his shoulder and neck and bit as well. Teeth that were suddenly as sharp as needles punctured his skin, but the taste of him drowned out everything but Burke. He howled as he stiffened, and she felt him spurting, felt his cock swelling within her as he flooded her with seed.

Heat filled her, the places where their skin touched inordinately sensitive as he held her tight, coming with great gasps.

When he finally relaxed, she was too sated to do more than

rest in his arms and blink up at him.

"That was just the beginning."

She smiled, startled though pleased and excited when her body stirred yet again.

"Burke."

"Hmm?" He rotated his cock within her, and she groaned as his fading erection suddenly stiffened again.

"I think I've found my inner beast."

Burke knew a sense of belonging he wanted to experience forever. Granted, he had family, acceptance and a duty to his town. But Rachel in his arms felt different. She made him feel...whole. The feline within her begged for release, and he knew their sex would only grow more passionate and more out of control, her heat attracting males far and wide since he'd opened the lid on her Ac-taw desires. Before, Rachel had been in and out of heat, unpredictable and hell on his needy cock. But now... now she was open and calling to him on a level he couldn't refuse.

She'd taken him, *bitten him*, and he needed to claim her as part of his pride before any other Shifters wandered too close. She belonged to him, dammit, and he refused to share her with the wolves and foxes already sniffing around her. Hell, he didn't want to share her with anyone, and he knew he had to.

"*Dean, Grady*," he sent with a growl, the mental pathway difficult in his human form. "*I need you here for the marking. Don't bother dressing.*" He felt their excitement purring deep in his mind.

His brothers had remained near, patrolling the grounds when Burke wasn't around to do it. Tonight he'd taken longer at the ranch than he'd thought, and almost hadn't made it out, so he'd sent Grady ahead of him to spell Dean, the three of them, plus Joel, working in shifts to see to Rachel's protection.

"Rachel?" Burke rested his palms on her ass, the wall, more than him, holding her up. He was extremely aware of his come sliding down her legs and over his thighs. Her wet heat surrounded him, and he had to resist the urge to start pumping again. He sniffed and was surprised to find he'd done a decent job of starting the claiming. Hell, she smelled of him already, his marker lingering despite his intent to wait to mate with her.

Burke had known since that walk by the stream, but this joining reaffirmed it. He would take Rachel to mate. In his entire life, he'd never desired another with such intensity, never had such loving feelings for a woman the way he did for Rachel. His beast wanted her, the man wanted her, and he would move heaven and hell to have her. But first he needed her to be feline, and to make her so as quickly as possible. As difficult as he expected it might be for him to accept it, he needed his brothers' help.

"Burke, what's wrong?"

He realized he'd missed half of what she'd said and gave her a wry grin. "I'm not thinking too clearly right now, you'll have to forgive me." She laughed, then groaned when he hitched her higher over his cock. "Rachel, I have to mark you. Tonight."

She stared at him, not seeming angry, worried or scared as he'd anticipated. "Why?"

"Because I need to. I *have* to." He frowned, knowing it was coming out all wrong. But he didn't know how to explain his urgency without admitting he meant to mate with her. Coming off her divorce, she'd explained she wasn't too keen on men, and he hadn't been offended, just relieved to know he'd done nothing more than growl at Sarah to piss her off. That Rachel had let him get this far gave him high hopes. But that didn't mean he assumed she'd be easy to bring down. Rachel had a crafty edge to her, a perfect fit for a catamount, or a silver fox sniffing too close. Fucking Gerald. Jealousy rose again at the thought of how often she'd seen the fox.

What if she was starting to lean toward Gerald and his clan? But Burke couldn't afford to move too quickly, not if he wanted all of her. He had to watch how much he admitted to needing her until he had her hooked on the taste of him, on the smell of him, so as not to scare her off.

"You have to?" She squeezed him inside her and he moaned, helpless to resist her approaching lips and devouring kiss.

When he could breathe again, he tried explaining what he intended with the marking when her eyes widened, her stare centered on a presence over his shoulders.

"Grady and Dean." He sighed and withdrew from her body, still holding her in his arms. "We need to mark you, Rachel. You're mine—ours. You know it and I know it." He couldn't control his dominance as he pushed her to submit.

Her eyes flashed and his hunger rose. Passion flared in the green depths of her gaze, and her musk permeated the room. Feline excitement, a surge of pheromones telling them she was more than ready, if not yet willing. "You want me to have sex with *your brothers*?"

Burke hissed and his brothers took a step back, giving him space. "No, I don't *want* you to fuck my brothers. I *need* you to do it. All three of us marking you together will ensure your beast is feline. And you'll be one of ours to protect." *To love.*

"Um, I know I was kind of wild, but I've never done threesomes or, ah, a foursome before." She swallowed loudly, but her pupils dilated with lust.

"Much as I wish it could be this way all the time," Grady

rumbled, "I have a feeling big brother is only allowing us this one night."

"You're damned right." Burke flashed his teeth in warning, and Rachel's breathing increased.

"Oh." She rubbed against him and it was all he could do not to fuck her against the wall again. Glancing at Dean, he noted the desire burning in his brother's gaze. Grady, too, looked ready to pounce, his body hard, burning with need.

"Take her into the bedroom." Burke forced himself to relinquish his hold on her, handing her into Grady's waiting arms. But watching her squirm in his brother's hold wasn't as difficult as Burke had thought it might be. Instead, a peculiar calm descended over his raging excitement, and a primitive instinct to bring Rachel to all the Chastells before claiming her as his own consumed him. This would make her family, and cement the ties between his future mate and his brothers.

Burke quickly followed them into Rachel's room, only to see her on her back in the middle of her bed. Her eyes were closed in bliss, her body arched, supplicant, as Grady and Dean laved her breasts with their mouths.

"So eager, hmm?" He surprised himself by chuckling, but soon lost his humor as his own needs rode him hard. Grady ran his hands over her body while he toyed with her breast, and his fingers unerringly sought and entered her pussy. Dean left her breast to kiss her mouth, and Rachel's clever little hand wrapped around his brother's dick, pumping and squeezing and turning Dean into a raging animal.

"*Yes.*" He thrust against her thigh, pushing more into her hand. "That's it, baby. Squeeze me harder. Oh yeah. More."

Grady groaned, and Burke couldn't help fisting his own cock as he watched his brothers fuck his mate. The marking musk permeated the room, all three of them desperate to cling

189

to Rachel's feminine wildness, to her ability to soothe and fight and love like a true Ac-taw.

"God, I want to come inside her." Grady stared up at Burke through a slitted gaze, asking permission.

Burke's beast raged, but his human half wanted to share her love, wanted his brothers to know the warmth he'd found. "Rachel?"

Dean broke from her mouth and Burke's breath caught. Her eyes had fully changed, yet her body remained human. "Burke, help me. I'm so hot. I need, so badly."

"Rachel, all this. It's not too late to say no." Dean and Grady stared at him as if he'd lost his mind. And maybe he had. "We're going to come inside you, Rachel. All of us. Everywhere." His cock throbbed at thoughts of her ass, of sinking deep inside her flesh and possessing every ounce of her. "Your body is begging to be shown its inner beast. You're in heat but you're not ovulating, so we aren't going to procreate, but we need to thoroughly mark you. And the fastest, easiest way to do it is through our come."

Rachel arched into Grady's hand cupping her breast. "Oh, Burke, Grady." She turned to face Dean, her body feverish and glistening with sweat under the dim light of her room. "Dean. I want you all so much. I can't think. I'm empty, Burke. You left me too soon."

Burke joined them on the bed, their weight easily filling the large, king-sized monstrosity Charlotte had left to Rachel. "Baby, you might not know it yet, but I'm never leaving you again."

His brothers stared at him in shock, but he didn't care. He was keeping Rachel, and he'd as good as declared himself. Grady's mouth quirked and he exchanged a look with Dean.

"You know, bro, we'd better take full advantage of tonight.

He'll never let it happen again."

Dean's eyes shone in the darkness. "Oh yeah. I just hope tonight doesn't ruin me for other women. She tastes so sweet."

"So much power, and her clawing feline is like a drug."

Burke settled between her thighs, inhaling his scent over hers. He shoved Grady's fingers aside and licked her clit, sucking on the small bud. In a low voice, he murmured, "Her pussy is addicting. Enjoy tonight, guys, because it won't happen again. Not with my future mate."

He didn't think she'd caught what he'd said. By the look of her, Rachel was in another world, desire turning her into the creature she'd been born to be.

"What are we waiting for, then?" Grady asked, smiling through his elongated teeth. "On your hands and knees, Rachel. We've got a surprise for you."

Chapter Six

Rachel's entire world centered around the heat between her legs. Her body felt like one giant mass of nerves, and every stroke of Grady and Dean's raspy tongues was setting her ablaze. She squirmed against them, fighting because it made the scent in the room sweeter.

Large hands turned her onto her belly, propping her up on her hands and knees. And then a powerful fist grabbed her hair and jerked her head up, so that she stared at Burke's domineering hold.

"We're going to take you now, baby. Hard and fast, and slow and long. And we're going to fill you with come. To mark you."

She moaned, wanting them. Nothing existed but Burke and his brothers using her, taking her to places she'd never before been. She couldn't stop looking at Burke even as she felt one of them mount her from behind, spreading her knees apart. He slapped her ass and thrust deep, and she shook with the force of his penetration.

"That's it, Grady. Give it to her. She needs it, don't you, baby?"

The want built, her pussy clenching and drawing Grady deeper.

"Fuck, yes," Grady hissed, pumping as he clenched hard fingers into her hips.

"And now Dean." Burke let her go and moved aside, and Rachel found herself staring at Dean's large cock. Thinner than Burke's, his shaft was just as long and beautiful. Slick with the precome beading at his tip, his rod was golden, like the rest of him, but flushed from desire. "Suck him off, Rachel. Swallow him, and then swallow me."

She moaned and opened her mouth, accepting Dean as he pushed gently between her lips. Nothing registered but the salty, male taste of him. She wanted this so badly, to belong, to bring pleasure as she'd experienced with Burke. And knowing he watched made it all the more erotic.

Glancing to Dean's left, she saw Burke on his knees pumping his cock with his hand, his face tight with arousal as he watched her getting fucked by his brothers.

Grady felt huge taking her from behind, and she surprised herself by not gagging when Dean shoved deeper into her mouth. The glorious feeling of possessing and being possessed intensified when a heavenly scent descended over them all, and she felt her chest vibrate as she worked Dean's cock.

"Shit, she's purring," Dean moaned and thrust harder. "Oh fuck, Rachel. I'm going to come, baby."

"I can't last much longer," Grady rasped.

Dean cursed and jetted into her mouth, and Rachel swallowed him, licking his shaft clean before tonguing a few drops of come from his taut sac.

"God, that was good," Dean sighed before being dragged back.

"Now me," Burke demanded, and Rachel eagerly opened her mouth to accept him. She took his thrusts easily, his tight hold on her hair turning her on even more. The thought of being wanted so much by three sexy men was such a turn on. Behind her, Grady had to be leaving bruises from his grip on her hips, but his cock kept bumping her pleasure spot and she came, pushing him into an orgasm as well.

"Christ," he groaned and continued to come, even as she tightened around him.

"That's it, baby. Take him inside you. That's good, isn't it? And it'll be even better once you swallow my load as well. Then we're going to get to the good part. And I'm going to fuck that pretty little ass of yours." Burke's speech grew thicker, his breath raspier as he described in detail what he planned.

She was still quivering from her climax with Grady when Grady pulled out and crawled next to her. He lay down on the bed, and Dean shoved inside her.

"Take him," Burke ordered, groaning as he slid in and out of her lips. "You have the most fuckable mouth. And that stroke of your tongue…"

She fondled Burke's balls with one hand and heard him curse. He seemed to get harder, if that were possible. Dean fucked her, reaching around to toy with her plump clit, the nub bursting with sensation. Though he'd already spent once, Dean quickly worked himself toward orgasm again, his cock hot and tight within her. Rachel glanced at Grady to see him jerking off as he watched, his beautiful body straining. When her eyes met his, he whispered her name and rose to his knees, sliding his dick over the middle of her back. Burke began coming in her mouth, and Dean shot and yelled, his climax washing over him.

Burke slid another shot of come down her throat before easing out of her, and she closed her eyes, thoroughly spent. Dean remained inside her, his hands stroking her ass, and she felt warm jets of fluid hit her back as Grady came all over her. He rubbed it in, marking her, she supposed, her eyelids impossibly heavy.

"Let's give her a rest." Burke's deep voice sounded thick with satisfaction. She opened her eyes to see him lying before her, like a sated cat after its bowl of cream. "Oh, don't worry, Rachel. We're not done yet. That was just round one."

She groaned and the others laughed. Dean withdrew and eased her onto the bed, his warm hands rubbing her back, and pushing more moisture over her. She glanced over her shoulder to see him milking threads of semen from his cock to her back.

"Like lotion," she murmured, exhausted.

"But it has what you need," Grady said hoarsely next to her. "Our marking scent all over you. God, Rachel, I'm spent, but I want to fuck you all over again. You're so damned sexy."

Burke rumbled, and soon she heard low purring all around her. They sat beside her, over her, next to her, rubbing against her with human flesh and soon with golden fur. For what felt like forever she lay in a daze while they allowed their fur to press her soft skin. Not sure how much time had passed when she roused to consciousness, she opened her eyes to find three cougars fixated on her body, their noses in the air as if scenting something she couldn't.

Grady rumbled in a low bass. *"Damn, you're already marked."*

Rachel stared at him in awe, blinking wide awake. "Did I just hear that, or am I overtired and imagining things?"

"No, you heard it." Dean sounded mournful. *"We marked you."* He turned to Burke and rubbed his head against his brother's shoulder. *"Come on, Burke. It's just one night. That was way too tame for a proper marking, anyway."*

"Yeah, Burke. A whole night. That's what we agreed on." Grady stopped purring, waiting for Burke's reaction.

"*I don't like it, but I understand it. Now you need to ask Rachel.*"

Three sets of eyes turned to Rachel, and she swallowed loudly. "You want to do it again?" Again? Were they inhuman? Duh. Of course they were. A stirring in her womb stunned her into admitting that she was just as inhuman. Three men—three Shifters—and Rachel. Surely a fantastic night to remember. She glanced at Burke, and without understanding how, *saw* him soften though his expression didn't change.

"*It's okay, baby. This is natural, and much as I dislike to call your attention to it, most female catamounts are polygynous.*" Burke took human form again, his fur gracefully melting into flesh, his feline shape shifting smoothly into a man's.

Grady followed, shifting back. "That means they like more than one dude for sex," he explained to Dean, who growled before shifting back as well.

He punched Grady in the chest. "I know that, asshole. I can't spell worth a damn, I admit, but I'm not an idiot."

Rachel chuckled and her heart swelled at the warmth, at the familial banter between brothers. And she felt ten feet tall at the tender look in Burke's eyes.

"Well, Rachel? What will it be?"

"I think I love you."

Burke and the others froze.

Realizing what she'd admitted, she quickly recovered. "All of you, I meant. You're my family now, aren't you?"

Dean and Grady beamed, but Burke's satisfied smirk worried her. "Yeah, baby. We're your family now. But brothers we ain't."

Dean snickered before leaning down to kiss her. More hands touched her breasts, her clit, her ass... And then no one was laughing anymore as desire pitched anew.

The next day, Rachel woke to throbbing canines, a sore ass, and a tender vagina. But her mind was clear as a bell. She felt herself turn three shades of scarlet as last night came tumbling back in all its glory, and she covered her eyes with her forearm. Hell, but she'd taken *three men* to bed. Had even taken it in the ass, which hadn't been nearly as pleasant as she'd heard it could be. Of course, when Dean had kissed her all better she hadn't complained. And being the meat in a Burke and Grady sandwich had certainly whet her appetite.

"I'm a nympho." How the hell did she get back on track with her life after having experienced wild animal—thank God not literally "animal"—sex?

"I hope so. I love chicks who can't say no." Burke stroked her belly, and she stared at him in shock, having thought herself alone. He leaned up on one elbow as he caressed her. "Grady and Dean had a tour to take care of this morning. Poor guys. You wore them out and then they had to haul ass into Whitefish by ten." His grin was wide enough to make the big bad wolf cringe, and she excused herself for the poor analogy.

"Um, Burke? You're okay with all this?"

Burke came off his elbow to blanket her with his body. "The question is, are you okay with it, my beautiful nympho?" He nipped at her earlobe, causing a shudder of need to pass through her.

"I'm, I..." She exhaled heavily and smelled Burke with vivid senses. The sweet smell that reminded her of sex on a stick now had several other faculties to it. She could taste his satisfaction, could smell the aroma of his pleasure as his hand crept to fondle her breasts.

"God, I had you all over the place last night and I still want

197

you." He inhaled the skin below her ear and began purring. "I can't get enough of you, Rachel."

She wanted to reject her over-amorous body but couldn't. Burke, bless him, met her needs with a gentleness she would never have expected, and his soft petting after their blissful climax had her falling so deep in love that she had a hard time remembering why she'd sworn off men for a while.

"Rachel." He pressed his lips to the top of her head. "I'm so glad you came to us. You belong in Cougar Falls, with us." *With me,* she swore she heard whispered in her mind. She could feel him smiling into her hair.

But what struck her the most about the past few days was how much she'd come to care for Burke. She wanted to belong to him—to his pride, she hastily amended. *Oh hell. If I can't be honest with myself, who can I be honest with? I love him, and it scares me to death.*

"Baby, you okay?"

Her nerves must have shown on her face, and she hurried to cover her exposure. She shot him a broad smile. "Okay? My body feels like rubber, my brain like Jell-O, and I finally have you all to myself. What could be better?"

He began purring—God, how she loved that—and she found herself joining the rumbling sound. That quickly, contentment settled, her fears fading to the back of her mind. The pounding of Burke's heart increased in volume, and she instinctively sniffed, trying to understand his emotions.

"Oh, yeah." He chuckled and stroked a hand over her hair. "You're ready to shift, Rachel. By marking you we finally woke you up. What say we go outside and give you some space. The first change is going to be hard, but I'll help you through it." He rose, heedless of his nudity, and pulled her with him. "Dean and Grady are going to be pissed they missed this."

She followed him blindly, her attention caught by the myriad scents pressing to be identified. Gerald's fragrance lingered in the house, subtle underneath Grady's, Dean's and of course, Burke's overpowering marker. Like a heady cologne, Burke's scent made her want to rub her face and body all over him. Taking him into her, as if claiming him as her own.

Burke opened the back door and took her with him, and she had a moment's hesitation at being naked on the back lawn.

"Don't worry. I don't sense anyone else around. It's just you and me, two cats ready for a good time." His wide, satisfied grin made her smile. "I am so fucking happy right now. You have no idea."

His joy was contagious, and she leapt into his arms, hugging him close. "Maybe I do."

Burke's happiness deepened into something more, and his body hardened in excitement. "Damn. Sorry about that. With you, I can't stop myself from wanting sex."

Right. Sex. Nothing more. Not that love lingering in his gaze, or the pitter patter of loving anticipation fluttering in my belly. Just sex.

Rachel disengaged against her protesting glands and took a deep breath. "Okay. So show me how to shift. Or change, turn. Whatever it is that you do. Show me."

"Don't be nervous. Just do what I do. Follow with your eyes and your mind."

She frowned, not quite understanding. But as Burke slowly shifted, she mimicked his movements. And then she began hearing soft commands in her mind that she accepted as well. Her skin itched and her bones ached. She moaned as unfamiliar stretching caused pain, and as her bones and muscles realigned, her moans turned into soft whines, feline

199

cries for help.

Instead of Burke's voice, however, she heard his thoughts in her mind and read impressions from his body language that spoke so plainly she couldn't believe she'd never noticed how expressive a cat was before.

"Let it come. Embrace your inner beast. Easy, love. Just relax."

He'd done that last night too. Called her "love". Her attention diverted, she found it easier to do as he said and fell into the changes in her body with little resistance, accommodating the pain.

"Very, very nice." Burke rubbed his head against hers, and the press against her whiskers made her want to sneeze. *"Sorry. You'll learn to recognize shifts in pressure and scents, so pay attention to those whiskers and that powerful nose. Open your mouth, baby."*

She did and managed a yawn of sorts that felt wider than anything she'd managed as a woman.

"Beautiful set of teeth." He grinned, his eyes slanting and his lip curling slightly. *"Sarah will be so jealous. You can tear her up with one big bite if you want."*

"So does raptor taste like chicken?"

Burke chuffed, the feline equivalent of a laugh. *"By all means, when you chew her up, let me know."*

"Maybe I will." Having tasted and shared sex with Burke, Rachel felt more than possessive. Burke was hers now, and Sarah Duncan had better learn to keep her hands, talons, and whatnot off Rachel's lover.

He pushed her with his head toward the bordering woodline near his property. *"Let's run for a bit and let you adapt to your new body."*

Minutes turned into an hour as Rachel ran on four paws, her tail a balancing guide as she played, racing in the woods with Burke. Overjoyed to be sharing this first with him, she shared with him everything she experienced.

"*It's like a rebirth, this feeling.*" She meant the shift, but she realized much of what she felt she could attribute to Burke, to his genuine spirit and selfless devotion.

"*It is. I remember the first time I shifted.*" They settled around a small stream that widened into a watering hole. "*I had just reached my thirteenth year. My voice was changing, my body was gangly and reed-thin. But my senses were on overload, you know?*"

Did she.

"*And when I shifted, it was as if I'd been given a special pair of glasses, like I could see so much of life that had until then been passing me by.*"

"*That's nice. The perfect way to describe what I'm feeling. You know, Burke, you have these great moments of poetic clarity that just don't seem like they should be coming from a six-four ranch hand.*"

He laughed. "*Yeah, my brothers like to give me a hard time for being so insightful. Drives them nuts, me always being right.*" He gave her a shrewd glance. "*Nothing much throws you, though, does it? Not this shifting, the marking last night or even the knowledge that this town and the people inside of it are real.*" He shook his head. "*You're amazing, Rachel. And I'm not the only one who thinks it. You might just have ruined my brothers for any other women after last night.*"

The embarrassment she should have felt didn't come. The beast within her acknowledged the marking she'd received as her due. "*Oh?*"

His eyes glinted and his scent rose to cover her. "*Yeah. You were so damned sexy under us, taking us inside you. But mostly they sensed your giving heart, your willingness to help others. It's that caring that gives you great power. That love that even your dickless ex couldn't stomp all the way out of you. You're Charlotte's niece for sure."*

She warmed all over, and her heart took another dip in his direction. *"I just hope I can live up to her, and your, expectations."*

"You will, baby. Hell, you already have." His gaze at that moment looked entirely human in a cat's body. *"Rachel, I have to tell you something. I—"* He stopped and stared over her shoulder, his eyes narrowing. *"Stay by my side unless I tell you to go back to the house. We've got company."*

As he said it, a foul odor assaulted her. Foreign canines intruding on her land. She growled low in her throat, wanting them gone. Spores of threat contaminated her peace, breaking this meaningful interlude with Burke, and her anger grew.

"Damn, Rachel, tone it down. That mean streak in you is a serious turn-on."

Shocked that he could tease in the face of danger, she snorted in response but felt her fury subside a little. *"You're not helping my inner beast that wants to rip their throats out."*

"You're right. I'm helping you control yourself. This isn't the way I wanted to introduce you to your wild nature. But when threatened, your instincts prevail. Just remember, you're catamount. These fucking dogs are nothing more than leftover hamburger."

She smacked her lips and he chuckled.

"Don't let them throw you. Stand strong, right next to me, and we'll get rid of them. Remember, this is your land. And the totem is yours as well."

"Don't you mean the town's?"

"*No. It's yours to protect, just as it's my job to protect you.*" He stared into her eyes, the golden glow of his gaze sincere. "*Nothing is more important to me than you, Rachel. Nothing.*"

Oh, God. Was he saying what he seemed to be saying? His body angled toward hers, keeping her both well guarded and well cared for. Under his tender gaze, she even felt loved, but couldn't tell if that was a reflection of her feelings for him or not.

It was all too soon. So many life-altering changes…and yet, Rachel knew deep in her heart that she loved him. Her beast cried out to make him aware, to mark him as thoroughly as he'd marked her.

Burke's eyes widened with shock. "*Rachel, that scent. Are you…?*"

He never finished his sentence, for at that moment, a half dozen wolves stepped in sight, their mouths wide with toothy grins, their gazes hard and hungry. Stopping a good twenty feet from both Rachel and Burke, they sniffed and began growling at Burke. Before they could do more, another wolf, this one larger and more silver than the others, joined them by the small pool of water.

"*Honored sister, we welcome you home,*" the large one said. Cocking his head, he studied her. "*I think, perhaps, my welcome is too late. You've been claimed by a catamount.*" The wolf's sigh was clear. Unlike the others, this one possessed an aura of dignity and carried himself like royalty. "*But that's of little consequence, really. I'm sorry to rush you, but you need to find our totem, now. There's a hunting party coming this way, and I have no idea when they're due to arrive. Could be today, could be tomorrow.*"

"*Like we can believe anything you lying dogs have to say.*" Burke's ears flattened and he hissed at the leader.

The wolves growled in response and stepped closer, until the leader barked at them to stop. Rachel caught a spicy scent from the lead wolf he seemed to be projecting intentionally. *"Don't be more of an ass than you already are, Burke. This isn't about defending your mate, or about my idiot brethren trying to overtake Cougar Falls. This is about protecting the town from invading humans. I'm not lying."*

Rachel took her eyes off the leader to watch Burke, and his sense of amazement washed over her like rain. *"Monty? Holy shit. I thought you were dead."*

The wolf shuffled on his paws. *"It's a long damned story. But not now. Time's wasting. On our blood bond, I'm telling the truth."*

Burke shook his head, snarled once more at the wolves flanking Monty, and turned to Rachel. *"Much as I wish it otherwise, he's not lying. It's go-time, Rachel. Now or never."*

Chapter Seven

Confusion filled Rachel on so many levels she didn't know where to begin. The wolf, Monty, was obviously a lost acquaintance of Burke's. But his comments about invading humans, about her being Burke's *mate?*

"*Rachel.*" Burke nudged her with his broad head. "*We have to find it. Do what Charlotte wanted you to do. Find your inner beast.*"

Hello, she already had. "*I'm standing on four feet aren't I? And don't tell me you've forgotten last night already.*" Glaring at Burke and Monty, who seemed to be grinning at them, she tried to concentrate. Aunt Charlotte had mentioned following her beast. Well, her inner beast had traipsed all over the damned woods after Burke and seen nothing resembling a twenty-foot-tall totem pole.

"*Monty, you can stay.*" Burke nodded toward the surrounding wolves. "*But the rest of them need to get the hell away. This is hard enough as it is. We don't need the extra pressure.*"

Monty gave a short bark and the others slunk back into the woods, leaving Rachel, Burke and Monty alone.

"*Want to tell me why anyone would want to go hunting right here in our town?*" Burke asked Monty.

"It's worse than that. A group of a dozen or so professional hunters is paying through the nose to bag some wolves, cougars and foxes promised them by a fucking traitor in the Gray Wolf clan. And we're not talking run-of-the-mill sports nuts. We're talking specialized killers with no qualms about murdering nonhumans."

"Shit."

"Exactly. The rogue made a deal with them to exterminate most of the Shifters a small faction of the Gray Wolf clan wants gone. With the totem lost, anyone can find this place. And once the town's finally been cleared, I'm assuming that faction will turn on the expendable hunters and any of the wolves not agreeable to the situation. You know how much wolves hate hunters. Anyway, I volunteered to find and keep safe the new guardian. Once the totem's in place and Rachel's under wolf control, a new Order can begin for the pack."

Rachel began to understand the danger they were all in, and she stepped instinctively closer to Burke, eased somewhat when their bodies touched.

Monty surprised her by shifting to human form. Tall and lean, he looked both haggard and incredibly strong. A handsome Shifter, he had dark hair threaded with silver and ice-blue eyes that promised honesty. He held his hands up in a sign of surrender. "I'm not the threat here. Look, if I had wanted the rogue's plan to work, I wouldn't have warned you about it. You know me, Burke. I'm the same brother I was all those years ago, no matter what's happened since. But I don't want the gray wolves taking over Cougar Falls, and I really don't want those damned humans tainting our town. You have to put the totem back in place."

Burke shifted into human form suddenly, but put his hand on Rachel's head, cautioning her to stay as she was. "Why should I believe you, Monty? You up and disappeared years ago. Not a word in all the time you've been gone." Funny, but Burke sounded hurt under his gruff disbelief. "I thought you were dead, and now here you are when the town's at its most vulnerable. How do I know this isn't some ploy to put your hands on the totem and get me out of the way so you can try to control Rachel?"

"Please. I could have ordered the wolves to stay, or I could have ambushed you an hour ago when you watched her make her first change." Monty huffed a breath and lowered his arms, crossing them over his chest, not a bit embarrassed about his nudity. Then again, when a man looked like he did, what did he have to be ashamed about?

"*Look away from him, right fucking now.*"

Shoot. She must have unintentionally projected her appreciation to Burke. "*I'm still a woman, Burke. You people really need to wear clothes, you know.*"

Monty stared at them curiously, and she realized he didn't understand them. "*He can't hear us?*"

"*Not when I use this particular pathway to talk to you. And don't change the subject.*" His hands were curled into fists, and she could smell his aggression.

"Burke, we don't have—"

"Yeah, yeah, Monty. No time for this. I fucking get it. *Rachel?*"

She glanced away from Monty. "*Look, I'm only human. Okay, so maybe I'm not. He's an attractive man. But he's not you.*" She stared into Burke's eyes, the need to tell him the truth overwhelming. It was almost as if Aunt Charlotte were there whispering ghostly encouragement. And that was plain weird. But like Burke had said, it was go-time. The truth needed telling.

"*I love you, Burke.*"

The change that overcame him was instantaneous. He flowed into his cougar form and touched his forehead to hers, his scent overpowering.

"*God, Rachel. I love you, too. I want to mate with you, I want to marry you. I want—*"

"Hell, Burke. You're both giving off some really strong scents. Do you have to do this right now?" Monty glared down at his rising erection. "Not all of us have a female to share in your happiness, you get my meaning?"

The human part of Rachel was embarrassed she'd forgotten about a naked Shifter standing so close. She kept her eyes glued to Burke, who now found his friend's nudity amusing. Men.

Burke directed his thoughts back at Monty, and she followed his mental pathway. "*Sorry, Monty. Rachel, baby, we're sure as hell going to get into this later. But right now I need you to tell us exactly what Charlotte said in her letter. And all of it this time. I know you've been holding back.*"

Rachel growled. "*So what if I've been holding back? What Aunt Charlotte proposed was nuts. Or at least, I thought it was crazy when I read the letter. She told me to stop dwelling on the past and have some wild and crazy sex with you.*"

Burke's shit-eating grin made Monty roll his eyes.

"*And she wanted me to marry you, Burke, because she thought you were heaven-sent.*"

"*Smart woman. Always liked Charlotte.*"

"*She also told me to find the totem before the town had major issues.*"

"But she didn't tell you where or how to find it?" Monty asked.

"*No. She said, and this is verbatim because it sounded odd to me, 'Trust yourself, look deep into your heart and follow your beast, for he'll show you the way.'*"

Burke and Monty exchanged a look.

"*He'll show you the way?*" Burke sounded excited. "*She's not talking about your inner beast.*"

"Seems to me like Burke's your beast, Rachel, especially if you're considering mating the pathetic feline." Monty chuckled at Burke's glare while Rachel stared at Burke in astonishment.

"*She did tell you to follow your heart,*" Burke added. "*And I'm your heart, aren't I, baby?*" His gentle voice had her pulse pounding, and a throbbing started behind her eyes.

"*Yes, you are. I love you.*" She realized again, her heart opening as she looked into Burke's beautiful golden eyes. She breathed heavily, as if she'd been running, and felt as if she might burst.

"Rachel? You okay?" Monty took a few steps closer but stopped when Burke swung his head toward him, hissing a warning. "Easy, Burke. I'm not poaching. Something's a little off here."

"*Rachel? Honey, you're starting to shift back. Are you all right?*"

She couldn't answer him. Immense energy vibrated along her spine, flowing down her limbs and into her brain as if she'd been plugged into something. She saw Burke's eyes widen before blackness overtook her, yet she remained alert.

A rainbow of sensation, red anger, yellow happiness, blue calm and more, streamed through her consciousness. Tentacles of power pulled her into a vast embrace, making her feel at one with everything around her. Animal cries mingled with the flow of life through nature, water rushing through trees and grasses, wind rushing through the sky, on which raptors and eagles flew with wild abandon.

She could feel Monty's surprise and growing pleasure, could sense Burke's overwhelming love, lust and worry as he hovered protectively over her. The presence of other cats filtered, Grady and Dean in their animal forms rushing to her side. Time passed and more Ac-taw arrived. Wolves, foxes and bears, raptors and eagles. Animals gathering to celebrate life. Her inner beast stirred, and she felt her body completely return to its feline form.

"*Rachel, wake up.*" Burke nudged her with a large paw, and this time she opened her eyes. Directly before her, amidst a grouping of trees that had before been quite normal, stood a tall relic throbbing with power. The ancient carvings on the totem showed different animals blending one into the other, with the cougar reigning over all with wisdom and fierce devotion. Like Burke, she thought and smiled.

"*You did it, Rachel.*" Dean purred and rubbed against her neck. "*You found it again.*"

"*Way to go, honey.*" Grady shoved Dean out of the way and took over Dean's affectionate petting.

From behind her new family, dozens of Shifters howled their approval, beaming at Rachel as if she'd saved them from a fate worse than death. Which, come to think of it, she had.

"*Congratulations,*" Monty sent her, having changed back into wolf form. He cocked his head at Burke, who blinked lazily and took a step back from Rachel. She waited with curiosity as Burke actually allowed Monty—a male not his brother—to sidle next to her and rub under her chin with his muzzle as if seeking acceptance.

"*My bond brother,*" Burke explained. "*He's one of us, even though he's wolf. Kind of like Joel and Maggie, but a lot closer.*"

And that was good enough for her. She returned the

affection and saw Monty's toothy grin.

"*Now how about a celebration, Chastell style?*" Burke roared to the crowd. "*Come on over to my place and we'll throw one hell of a party.*" He turned to Grady and murmured something she couldn't quite hear.

Everyone began making noise again, and Rachel let Burke lead her away back toward the house.

"*Is it safe to leave it there in the woods?*" she asked, referring to the totem.

"*It's as safe as you are. The power to conceal it or to make it appear is yours and yours alone. I don't know what Charlotte was thinking not to have shown you all this years ago.*"

They began running toward the house, Rachel following her heart, her beast, with contentment and still a small measure of worry. "*But what if the rogue wolves try to steal it?*"

Burke chuckled. "*Are you kidding? The minute any of them try to touch the thing, it gives off a very ugly vibe. Like an electric shock. You and your protectors are the only ones allowed to touch it.*"

"*I still have a lot to learn about all this, don't I?*"

They reached her house and Burke shifted into human form, urging her to do the same. She did so easily, stunned at how simple the transformation was with Burke and the totem's magic telling her what to do. The minute she changed, Burke swept her into his arms and into the house. He didn't stop until they reached her bedroom, where he set her down in the middle of the bed.

Standing over her, he placed his hands on his hips and glared. "We don't have a lot of time before we need to join the others. So let's have the truth. You'd better not have been screwing with me out there, Rachel. You said you loved me."

She smiled, a catlike grin full of lust and affection. "I'm not sure. Maybe you should remind me of how much I have to gain by loving you."

Burke narrowed his gaze and pounced. She squealed with laughter and hugged him to her. "I love you, Burke. More than I ever thought I could possibly love anyone."

He inhaled her scent at the crook of her neck and nipped lightly. Trailing his lips from his bite to her ear, he stirred a path of heat that soon built into a bonfire in her womb. "Good, because we're mating, Rachel. And I'm never giving you up. No other women, no other men, not even my brothers," he emphasized, squeezing her tight when she mock-groaned in protest. "Sharing you was really hard."

He kissed her lips, drawing her breath deep into his mouth. "But loving you is so damned easy. I'll have to thank Charlotte every day for the rest of my life for leaving her stuff to you."

Rachel smiled against his lips. "So does that mean you're no longer interested in my property?"

"Keep the house and this plot for our grandkids. The only property I want right now is between those luscious thighs." Burke kissed his way down her body, lingering on her breasts as he sucked her nipples into hard peaks. His hands were everywhere, his mouth following suit. And then he had her legs spread wide, his mouth over the hottest part of her.

"I thought we had to join the others."

"They can wait. Any last requests?" he murmured, his breath torture over her aroused and moist clit.

"Love me, Burke." Her eyes welled with tears of joy. "Make me yours."

His scent, thick and sexy, fell over her in a huge wave, until she could no longer differentiate him from her.

"Honey, you've been mine since you walked into that damned diner with a chip on your shoulder." She was surprised to see his eyes glossy as well. "I love you, Rachel. All of you, forever...on just one condition."

She stared at him, embracing the lust and love consuming her. "Condition?"

He sucked her clit hard, drawing the nub between two suddenly very sharp teeth. The pleasure pain was exquisite before he let go. "Yeah. On the condition that you never look at Monty naked again."

She laughed before he resumed his carnal worship of her body. Groaning, she gave him his answer. "Anything for you, Burke. Anything."

About the Author

To learn more about Marie Harte, please visit www.marieharte.com. Send an email to Marie at marie_harte@yahoo.com or join her Yahoo! group to join in the fun with other readers as well as Marie at http://groups.yahoo.com/group/M_Hgroup.

GREAT
CHEAP
FUN

Discover eBooks!

THE FASTEST WAY TO GET THE HOTTEST NAMES

Get your favorite authors on your favorite reader, long before they're
out in print! Ebooks from Samhain go wherever you go, and work with
whatever you carry—Palm, PDF, Mobi, and more.

WWW.SAMHAINPUBLISHING.COM